THE TRAPPING

THE TRAPPING

Anthony Vela

To order additional copies of this book, contact:
Xlibris Corporation
1-888-795-4274
www.Xlibris.com
Orders@Xlibris.com
20698

This is for Victoria, who said I should do this—so I did.

And many thanks to all those who helped me along the way.

The journey is far from over.

Mark 10:8

AND THE TWO SHALL BECOME ONE FLESH;
so they are no longer two,
but one flesh.

CHAPTER ONE

O utside of the newly opened Southwick Museum, a line of people hungry for art ran around the white stone building. The museum had been created to bring in the city crowd that vacationed in the surrounding towns. Most of the townspeople had protested the museum, but they changed their tune when they found out the yearly revenues—some even bought every art history book they could find.

Gabe stood with the rest, waiting to get in. Wind swirled his hair across his face, a few loose strands sticking to his oily forehead. A sea of black birds dipped and dived between and around the tall smokestacks that stood amidst the open farmland of Southwick, New York. One enormous bird broke from the flock, floated down, and landed at Gabe's feet. He looked down with clenched fists, the hair on his back standing ready. The bird nodded a few times. A thin ashen streak ran down the top of its head and faded toward the middle of its back.

"Weetch himmm," it said.

"What the hell?" Gabe didn't blink.

The bird nodded once more and flew off to join the others. Gabe watched, mouth wide open and fists still clenched, as the sea

of black flew out of sight. He turned and looked back at the crowd—
nobody had noticed.

Gabe shook his head and spotted Mr. Burke—a burly man
whose face had more lines than a road map. He owned and worked
at Burke's Pharmacy. His grandchildren stood in line with beanie
babies clutched between their delicate fingers.

Mr. Brown and his wife Emily stood in front of Gabe. He
couldn't help but notice her blue-colored scarf as it ruffled in the
breeze.

"Is that you, Arthur? I haven't seen you in months. Do you
know, Thomas and I still have the portrait you painted of us hanging
above our living room couch? You wouldn't believe how many
compliments we get over it." Emily looked into her husband's
peanut-sized hazel eyes.

Gabe disliked being called by his middle name but he smiled
anyway. "Well, I'm glad you like it. I enjoyed painting it."

"You sure can paint, but boy did my neck stiffen up after you
finished it. But it was worth every bit of pain, right, Emily?" Mr.
Brown smiled at his wife, a glint in his eye. Gabe could see love in
Mr. Brown's smile and wished he had some in his own life.

"You must be crazy about this new museum," Emily said,
fixing her scarf. "How's your mother doing? You know, I'd still like
to come out and see her. That is, if you would like me to."

"Yes, the museum is just fine, and as for my mother, well, I
don't think she'd agree to it." Gabe shook his head.

"That's too bad. I really feel that a couple of therapy sessions
could do a world of good for her. Just like I said when you painted
my portrait, you can give me a call any time you like and I'll make
an appointment to drop by."

"I'll run it by her." Gabe rolled his eyes. His thoughts then
turned back to the strange bird. He looked toward the sky and
then to the line of people. *I can't believe they didn't see it.*

A man cleared his throat.

"It's finally going to open," Gabe said with a smile.

The short museum director with a dark blue suit, slicked-
back hair, and a painted-on smile stood on the finely polished

white marble steps leading into the museum. "Welcome, everybody. I know you've been standing out here, waiting all morning. The doors will be opening in a moment." He paused and pointed to the silver doorway that sparkled in the sun. "If you have any questions, there will be an information desk to your right as you step in. We hope you'll enjoy your visit." He turned and walked back into the building.

"Well, Gabe, Thomas and I hope to see you again sometime soon." Emily looked at her husband and kissed him on the cheek.

"Yeah, I'll probably see you in the museum, if not around town." Gabe looked on and hoped to be that much in love when, and if, he ever did get married.

The museum doors opened, and Gabe's heart raced. He felt like he had to see everything at the same time. He rushed by the information booth, which already had a line forming like the one outside. Gabe stopped first at the realist section, which already had its share of people standing around snapping pictures and studying with an eye of which art critics in New York City would be jealous. Gabe didn't need to snap any pictures—he had studied these artists for the past three years at the Westwood College. Finally, he could see their work in person. Gabe's style could be likened to the pastel colors of Andrew Wyeth with the surreal openness and shadows of Dali. Gabe shook his head. The colors! Not to mention the thick brush strokes. Maybe someday his work would be in a place just like this.

Three days earlier, an article in the *Southwick Press* had listed which artists' work would be here today, but it hadn't said anything about Munch, so Gabe wasn't prepared to see the painting he just laid his eyes on—*The Scream*, hanging on a plain white wall under two spotlights. The soft light presented the painting's true colors like no picture he had ever seen in a book. He also looked forward to seeing the expressionist Van Gogh even though he didn't paint in either artist's style. He had always considered painters like them to be the real artists, which was something he hoped to be.

Gabe had to practically fight his way through a wall of people to get to *The Scream*, on loan from The National Gallery of Norway.

He could almost hear the screech coming from the distorted figure on the bridge. He stepped back to get a better view and bumped into someone. "Excuse me," he said as he turned around.

Gabe gazed into the girl's black-speckled blue eyes, and his heart began to flutter. She had eyes to die for. Her skin, white as snow, had patterns of light and dark cinnamon-colored freckles, and her black hair was neatly woven into a tight bun and held together with golden clips.

"So, how do you like the museum? Isn't it just cool?" She wiggled with excitement.

"It's beautiful," Gabe said, really referring to her. "This town doesn't have much going for it in the arts, but now with this new museum, I suspect the arts in Southwick will grow like sunflowers in late August." He paused and looked at the nameplate pinned on the girl's shirt just above her right breast. "Sara. My name is Gabe. Nice to meet you."

A tall man looked in their direction, but when he met Sara's gaze, he quickly turned away. Sara shook her head. Gabe shot a glance in the tall man's direction, but he had already walked away.

Sara said, "I see you like Munch. You know, we also have some of his wood cuts."

Gabe gazed at her and took a moment to answer. "Yeah, I'd love to take a look at them. I like lots of styles, and this museum is full of them. It's a dream come true. And I can come here any time I like."

"Are you a painter?" Sara rubbed the side of her leg.

"I am. I study art at Westwood College. Do you go to college?"

"College," Sara said with a shy chuckle. "Gee, I'm flattered that you think I'm going to college, but I still have a year left of high school." She looked at her watch and said, "Listen, I go on break in ten minutes. They're supposed to have this neat little restaurant on the other side of the museum. Would you care to join me for something to eat?"

Gabe stepped back, took a deep breath, and smiled. He could just about hear his mother saying, *Girls are no good, so you better stay away from them—unless you want a world of hurt.* "Sure, I'd love to."

"If you wait right here, I'll check with my supervisor just to make sure. Things are gonna be pretty crazy around here today."

Gabe looked on as she delicately danced away into the crowd until he could no longer see her blue-and-white dress.

Studying the Munch painting for a second time, he couldn't believe his luck. Sara was the most beautiful girl he had ever seen, and here she was asking him out. He wiped his sweaty palms on his pants as his blood raced. He blew what few relationships he had with girls in the past, but he swore that if this one did take off, he would handle it like a box of fine china. He belonged in *The Scream*, filled with a storm of emotion.

A hand touched his shoulder. Gabe turned. Sara had let her hair down. It went past the middle of her back and was shiny like silk. "I only have twenty-five minutes, so we'd better move."

The restaurant was designed to look like a Mondrain painting—straight lines painted in primary colors on the floor, walls, and chairs, and even the clothes and hats the workers wore had the same patterns, not to mention the tables.

"This is so cool," Gabe said as they moved along the line of those waiting to be served.

"Yeah, isn't it," Sara agreed as she too looked around. "So what do you want to be when you get out of college?"

"I want to be a painter some day. Well, I'm already a painter, but what I really want is to make a living at it," Gabe said, as they both moved up along with the rest of the line.

"Are you going for your Bachelor of Fine Arts?"

"Yes, I'm going for my B.F.A. I wanted to go to a New York City art school, and I could have, but I have to take care of my sick mother at home. Westwood isn't that bad, but it's not a city college." Gabe let out a deep breath.

"Oh, I'm sorry to hear that." Sara ran a hand through her hair. "Do you have any brothers or sisters?"

"No, I don't." Gabe frowned.

"Why don't we sit over there by the window. It's got a good view," she said.

They walked to the other side of the restaurant and sat down against a large window overlooking the grounds below. Yellow and orange marigolds were starting to pop up everywhere. Small spruce trees were green as grass, and the leaves on the oaks lining the entrance all the way from the street were starting to bud—in a few years they would be reaching for the heavens like the smokestacks of Southwick.

"So, what are you having?" he asked.

"I'm not sure. What are you having?" Sara looked down at her menu.

Gabe grinned. "I'm just gonna have a milkshake."

"I guess I'll have one too."

"Great, I'll get us two milkshakes and be right back."

A few minutes later, Gabe came back with their drinks.

"So, do you plan to go on to college after you finish up with high school?"

"I haven't thought much about it, though I guess I probably should." She snapped her head to the left to get the hair out of her face. "My father said he'll pay my way, but I'm not sure I'd like it. Heck, I don't even like high school. It's too restrictive. I think my father just wants me to go to college so I'd be the first in the family."

"So you have brothers and sisters?"

Sara paused.

Ah, he had just touched on something close to her heart.

"I have a younger sister, but my older sister died along with my mother in a car accident two and a half years ago. I almost lost my life as well." Sara slowly rocked back and forth.

"I'm so sorry."

"Thank you." Sara blinked.

"I can remember the day my grandmother was laid to rest. We had the funeral at her home like people used to do many years ago. Anyway, I was sad, but my grandmother always told me that we should celebrate a person's life rather than focus on the pain and loss of their death. I know it doesn't sound like much in the advice department, but it did help me out a couple of times."

"You know, after my sister died, there wasn't a night when I didn't dream about her. I can still see her little round face, her glowing blue eyes, and her beautiful red hair. I even swear till this day that she spoke to me that night when she was supposed to have already been dead," Sara said, raising her voice to talk over the loudness in the museum restaurant.

"Really?"

"Yes."

Sara sipped her milkshake through a tall white straw, and smiled.

He sipped his own shake and got some on his lip. When he started to wipe the corner of his mouth with the edge of his napkin, Sara burst out laughing. "What's so funny?" he asked, putting the napkin down.

"Oh, it's nothing," she said and laughed into her hand. "It's just that—well, it's just that you looked so funny the way you were wiping your mouth like that. It kind of reminded me of how my sister and I used to fool around when we ate dinner at our grandmother's house." Sara looked away slightly. Her laughter quickly faded like the dying note of a song.

Gabe turned to see what had caught her attention. The tall man stood as erect as the columns around him. Gabe turned back to Sara and saw a change. Her black hair was brown, matted, and stringy, her eyes green, and her skin dark.

"Would you excuse me for a minute? I need to use the bathroom," Sara said. She rose and quickly left.

"Wait, I . . ." But Sara was already gone. Gabe followed. *My God, did I see what I think I just did?*

He waited outside the entrance to the bathroom. He couldn't see her, but he could hear her talking. But to whom?

"I must be going crazy if the tall man is here. But I can't be crazy. I just can't be. He's only a dream . . ." Her sobs muffled whatever else she said.

Gabe walked back to the restaurant. What was Sara talking about?

A few minutes later she returned.

"Are you okay?" he asked as she sat down across from him. Gabe stared at her, but her face had changed back. *What's going on here*, he thought.

"I'm all right, it's just that . . . whenever I talk about my mother and sister, it always brings out the worst in me. I hope you'll forgive me, considering we met only a little while ago."

"You don't have to explain yourself to me." His eyes fluttered. "I wish there was something I could do for you."

"You already have," she said with a smile, then looked at her watch. "I've got to get back to work." She sipped the last of her milkshake and started to take some money out of her dress pocket.

"No, it's on me," Gabe said with a wave of his hand. "You can pay next time."

"Thanks. It was nice meeting you."

"When can I see you again?"

"Tomorrow. I'll be in the museum tomorrow."

For the second time, Gabe watched as she bounced away through the crowded museum.

CHAPTER TWO

Southwick now had two places its people could flock to on Sunday mornings: the church, to hear Father Honeycomb's sermon, and the new museum.

Gabe arrived at the museum at 8:45 the next morning, sitting in his car, listening to the latest Rolling Stones song. At the end of the song, the DJ commented on how this group would never die, even though Keith Richards looked like a walking corpse.

On his sketchpad, he drew the farmland, what little was left of it, that lay so serenely behind the museum. Most of the farms that stood here for generations were being sold off to land developers so they could build more houses and shopping centers. Trees, shrubs, and bushes filled the landscape as well as a variety of flowers that, when came time to bloom (Gabe recalled from past years), would make the area look like an impressionistic painting—with the subtle tones of a Monet and the broad strokes of a Van Gogh. He deeply inhaled the fresh air and smiled. He could just about draw Southwick's landscapes from memory. He started drawing at two years old and was the envy of most of his classmates. He sipped his bottled water and couldn't help but notice the black birds sitting on the power lines, crowing every so often in unison.

As he drew, one of the crows flew down from the wire and

landed on the hood of his car. Gabe saw that it was the same bird from the museum by its gray streak—only now the streak went past the middle of its back. Gabe pulled away.

The bird kept looking toward the museum. Gabe had forgotten how dull and lifeless their dark eyes looked, like a shark's eyes as it devours its prey. Without warning, many of the birds swooped down to sit on Gabe's car. The white Chevy Nova, which had so many rust spots that it looked like a leopard, was now covered with a sea of black. Gabe squawked, dropped his pencil, knocking his drawing pad to the floor, and quickly rolled up the driver's side window. He could feel his heart thumping. Not for a second did he look away.

When he was a kid, a friend of his, Charly Eaton, had been killed by a flock of black birds just like the ones sitting on his car now. They had stripped Charly to the bone like vultures on road kill. To this day, Gabe could hear the boy's horrid screams. Gabe had been the first one out there and had seen Charly's tattered corpse lying like a pile of wet rags with blood and bones showing through.

From the corner of his eye, Gabe saw the brief blur of a tall figure just inside the back door of the museum. He reached for the horn to scare the birds away, but they flew off on their own. He picked up his sketchpad and watched the birds fly back to the wire. They stayed there, watching over him like some evil paladin.

Seeing Sara, Gabe quickly stumbled out of his car, knocking over the cigar box of pencils, pens, and erasers. He left them and ran over to see her. "Sara," he called out, still running. "Sara, it's me, Gabe." She had just finished locking her bike to the bicycle rack.

Sara's dress fell just above her toes and was pleated around the waist, the color a bright white like fresh snow. Her black hair, neatly combed, contrasted with her white dress, and her lips were a shade of pink rose petals that highlighted her pale face. She wore no mascara, but her eyelashes were already as long as a daddy-long-legs. She had added a dab of cheek color to match her lips, and bronze eye shadow. The brown did just the right trick to show off her deep blue eyes, which sparkled like the sea.

Trying to catch his breath, Gabe sucked in enough air to be able to talk. High above, the black birds circled as if waiting for their next meal.

"Sara, it's me, Gabe," he managed to get out.

Sara looked as if saluting herself as she shielded her eyes from the sun, and smiled. "Gabe, what a pleasant surprise. I didn't expect to see you until later today." She tugged on her backpack. "I'd love to stay here and talk, but I'm already late for work. If you like, you can stop by about twelve thirty. If not, I'll be working till five o'clock." She started walking toward the museum, stopped, and looked up at the birds. "There they are again. For the past few days I can't seem to get away from them."

"I hate those birds," Gabe muttered. "You should have seen them before, when they landed on my car. If I never see another one for the rest of my life it wouldn't be too soon."

Sara shook her head. "I couldn't agree with you more." She continued toward the museum.

Gabe followed. "Where can I find you?"

She opened the back door of the museum. Gabe looked and saw a tall man in the shadow of the doorway who then backed away from the glass doors.

"I take lunch at twelve thirty, so if you can make it, I'll meet you right here." She pointed to the steps.

"Definitely."

Sara entered the museum. Gabe smiled and walked back to his car.

Gabe rushed home from the museum to attend to his ailing mother, Martha. He hated the fact that he had to take care of her, but asked himself every day who would when he decided to leave.

"Gabe, Gabe, is that you?"

"Of course it's me." Who else would it be?

He grabbed the morning paper, put on some coffee, and made sure the heat was set exactly to seventy degrees. If it was seventy-one or sixty-nine, she'd be in an uproar the rest of the day. Gabe knocked on her door and waited. He shook his head and remembered the last time he happened to barge in on his mother, four Easters ago, when she wasn't as sick as she was today. Gabe had made a basket for her filled with her favorite things: marshmallow eggs, black jelly beans, white chocolate, caramel popcorn in the shape of a bunny, and saltwater taffy—she just loved taffy. That morning, all Gabe had wanted to do was surprise her before she got up. He opened the door to her bedroom and quietly walked in holding the basket. A course of moans filled his ears as he stood motionless in his mother's room. "Mother, are you okay?" he asked, gripping the basket with white knuckles. A moment later, the moans subsided and Gabe could see someone else under the covers with his mother.

"Who's that?" a man demanded as the sheets ruffled. The man got out of bed naked and walked over to confront Gabe. "What are you doing in here, boy?" he asked after he caught his breath. He resembled an ape as he flared his nostrils, which were big to begin with, and puffed out his big hairy chest. Gabe half expected him to pound on that chest. Gabe's mother sat up in bed, pulling the covers up to her wrinkled neck, and closed her eyes.

"Didn't your mother tell you to stay out of her room when I'm in the house?" the naked man asked.

But Gabe just stood there, holding on to that basket as if his life depended on it. A large force hit him in the chest. He flew back, his head hitting the door. The basket crashed to the ground. Black jelly beans rolled all over the floor, as did the rest of the basket he had so elegantly made.

"Now, get out of here, boy," the naked man said, pointing.

Gabe looked up at him, gritting his teeth, but was afraid to strike back.

His mother remained silent. The man strutted back to the bed. Gabe's mother had turned and buried her face in the pillow.

"Come on in," his mother said. "And you better have my coffee brewing." Gabe reached for the light switch. "No. No lights. Especially since I just got up." Gabe didn't move, feeling like a soldier waiting for her next command. "Are you just going to stand there or are you going to hand over the paper?"

Gabe inched forward as if a monster lay in his mother's bed, which, in his mind, wasn't far from the truth. Gabe handed the paper to her. Why in the world did she want to read the newspaper? She hadn't been out of the house for God knew how long, and the only people she talked to, other than Gabe, were her sister, Jane B. Parker, and her only friend, Molly Sweet. And even visits from them were few and far between. Gabe thought they both must be very compassionate women. That, or just plain crazy.

"Why does it always have to be so dark in here?" he asked.

"Why do you always ask such stupid questions?" She turned on the only light she ever put on in the room: her reading lamp, which was clipped onto the side of her night table next to her bed. "You know that bright lights bother my eyes."

Martha unfolded the paper. She read it every morning from front to back, including the obituaries.

Gabe sighed. Her reading light shone brighter than the ceiling light—it looked like a night spotlight on a backyard porch.

"I think I hear the whistle blowing. I'll be right back."

Standing in the kitchen, he wondered, *When am I ever going to leave Southwick?*

As long as his mother was alive, he'd have to stay here and take care of her. It wasn't etched in stone but damned close to it. Gabe poured the water for her coffee and made sure to add just the right amount of whole milk, two heaping spoonfuls of sugar, and most importantly, two ice cubes. If he did anything less, he'd be chewed out like a child. He inhaled the steam, rising like mist off a spring lake.

"Here's your coffee," he said, trying to erase the smile from his face. With dark circles under her even darker eyes, Martha stared him down. She sipped the coffee and smelled its aroma. She smiled, ready to jump down his throat if it wasn't to her liking.

"I see you remembered the ice. That's nice of you," she said with a put-on smile that looked like the devil's. Anyone else would have been caught off guard, but Gabe had seen this sort of thing too many times to count. In fact, he was waiting for her next reply. He knew what she was going to say before she did.

"What the hell are you so happy about?" Martha asked so violently that she spilled her coffee onto the newspaper and bed sheets. "See what you made me do. Don't just stand there, get me something to clean this up with." Martha sat up all the way. For a moment, Gabe just stood there, but one look at his mother's twisted face was more than enough to get him moving. He went to the bathroom and wet a washcloth.

"I already got it," she yelled with a forked tongue. "What took you so long?" She finished blotting up the coffee with a towel from her night table.

"I'm sorry, Mother, but I've got so much work at school and I've been so tired lately." Complaining was the wrong thing to do, and he knew it. He just hoped she'd forgotten the question before the spill. That's all she had to hear—that he had his eye on a girl. She'd blow her cork like a bottle of New Year's Eve champagne.

"What would you like for breakfast?"

"Breakfast?" She pointed at him. "I'm not finished with you yet. You didn't tell why you had that clown's smile all over your kisser a moment ago."

When she wanted to, she had the memory of a mathematician.

Gabe walked over to the dresser. "Listen, Mother. It's not a crime to smile." He glanced at himself in the mirror and saw a taut face and staring eyes.

"No, it's not, but you still haven't told me why. Now, don't stand so far away from me. I won't bite. Come over here and let me see you," she said, waving him over.

Gabe slowly inched his way over to her.

"Closer still," she hissed.

Gabe now stood right next to her side of her bed. She breathed heavily. Her skin had changed to a ghostly white over time from being indoors every minute of the day. She looked more dead than alive.

"Don't lie to me, boy," she said, as her dark brown eyes nearly popped out of her head. "I've told you a thousand times before not to lie to me. You know that old saying about how a grown son can never lie to his mother without getting caught? Well, it's true! Because right now I can tell you're lying, which can only mean one thing," she said and turned away. "You're dating someone, aren't you?" She turned back, lip curled and her face creased.

"Yes, I am, Mother," Gabe said with a raised voice. "I can't stay here forever. My life is just starting, and I don't want to miss any more than I already have."

"You won't have to worry that much longer." His mother rearranged her pillows so that both of them were on top of each other behind her head. "The doctor called early this morning and told me I probably don't have long to live."

For a moment, Gabe felt the piano that his mother had become lifted off his back. He couldn't imagine not having to take care of her any longer, but he wasn't holding his breath. In the past she had lied about her health too many times to count. She would use guilt to control Gabe. It was the only thing she had left.

"What are you talking about, Mother?" He leaned over her. "The doctor must be mistaken. You look as good as ever."

"Are you saying I'm stupid and I don't know what someone told me? I'll have you know that my faculties are as good as they ever were. Now, you take back what you said and just maybe I'll forgive you. Come on, Gabe. Do as I say," she said with a frown.

"I'm sorry, Mother. If you say the doctor told you that, then it must be true. I'm really sorry."

This wasn't the first time she said she was dying, and it wouldn't be the last. As much as Gabe sometimes wished her dead, at others he wished he had gone away to college like he had wanted to.

Gabe blamed his father for her condition. Ever since he ran out on Gabe when he was a kid, his mother changed, and steadily regressed to what she is today. He cursed the ground his father walked on. He should share in this mess that his mother had become. Dealing with her death would be hard enough, but to be there every step of the way, watching her die a little at a time, was just not fair. He wasn't supposed to watch his mother die. He rubbed his forehead and looked down at her.

"You come here and give your mother a kiss," Martha said playfully as though nothing had happened. Gabe flushed. He bent down and kissed her on the forehead. She smiled and grabbed his hands. Her palms were moist, and her hands trembled as if she barely had the strength to hold on. Gabe placed her hands on the bed and held them tightly. Tears fell from his mother's dark eyes. She let go of Gabe, turned, and buried her face in her pillows. Gabe looked away and slowly left the room. He quietly closed the door and listened to her sobs and almost cried himself.

In the kitchen, he poured a glass of orange juice. He couldn't help but think about what Mrs. Brown had said yesterday at the museum. Mrs. Brown had wanted to come out to visit on several occasions, but Gabe always put a stop to it. He knew how his mother would react. But time was running out, and he no longer could provide the care his mother so desperately needed.

He gave Mrs. Brown a call and set up a day for her to come over. For the first time in a while, Gabe felt a deep relief. He started the wash and decided to wait until after dinner to tell his mother that Mrs. Brown would be coming over in a few days. He knew it would be easier to break the news to her after a good meal. Right now, she was already sad, and this would only cause her more grief.

###

Whenever he thought about Sara, a warm feeling filled his body. Sara had an aura about her, something Gabe couldn't put his finger on. He arrived at the museum, kicking up dirt as his car came to a skidding stop. The parking lot was filled, so he parked across the street. The sun was all alone in the cloudless sky, so he put on a pair of oval sunglasses. He walked around to the back of the museum. No sign of her. So he leaned on a large oak tree and waited. Gabe was late by only a few minutes and hoped she too was running behind. Kicking at the dirt, Gabe waited another ten minutes, and then another five. Now he fidgeted. Maybe she forgot. Or maybe he just missed her.

He walked over to see if Sara's bike was locked on the rack. He couldn't find any bike that looked remotely like hers, though he did see many of the popular mountain bikes so many kids rode these days. Gabe thought about going inside to find out what happened to her, but he didn't think it mattered at this point. Knowing what happened wouldn't change the fact that he couldn't have lunch with her. Even if she was inside, her lunch break would already be over. Shoulders hunched, Gabe headed back to his car. He left with a screech and a cloud of brown dust, tires burning as they hit the street. Maybe she went home sick. Then again, someone could have stolen her bike.

He was not in the best of moods as he pulled into his driveway and parked the car. He sat for a moment, not wanting to deal with his mother, but having no choice. Already well after her lunch time, he didn't have a second to waste. He flipped off the sunglasses, hung them on the rearview mirror, and got out of the car. Now he wished even more than ever that he had gone away to college.

"Do you know what time it is?" she yelled from the living room. "It's almost one thirty! Where have you been?"

"I went to that new museum to meet a friend." Gabe entered the living room.

His mother was sitting on the couch, which had fallen apart so badly that knitted blankets had been thrown over the back and sides to cover it.

"Does that friend happen to be your new girlfriend?" Martha asked, her dull, sunken eyes widening.

"Yes," Gabe said over the screaming television. His mother loved it loud.

"What did I tell you about girls? If you want a world of hurt, hook up with a girl," she said, running through the channels with the clicker. "Anyway, you're not ready for a girl. Look what happened with your last girlfriend. Mary Esher was her name, wasn't it?" she said with a snicker.

Gabe squinted hard. Mary Esher had indeed been his last girlfriend—a local girl who lived a few blocks away. He wasn't that good when it came to girls, but this one hadn't been his fault. Not in the least. He had seen Mary from time to time since the split, and every time he did, he felt embarrassed as he recalled the incident that led to the breakup. Gabe's mother now wore a shit-eating grin.

Behind Martha's house, a three-bedroom ranch with an unfinished basement and a garage off to the side, which was ready to collapse at any moment, timothy grass as high as an elephant's eyes covered a field the size of a small park. Mary and Gabe used to go through the field to Otto's lake, which they called "Sanctuary" because it was so peaceful and tranquil. One hot summer evening, when the sun was setting, Mary and Gabe had gone to the lake for a swim to cool off. When they got there, they realized they had forgotten their bathing suits. When Mary took off her shorts and shirt and stood in her underwear, Gabe stared and then took off his shirt and shorts. He left his underwear on, but Mary wouldn't have any of it. She stopped him before he could jump into the water.

"What's the matter?" Gabe asked.

"Nothing, but if you want to go for a swim with me, you're going to have to get rid of them." She pointed to his stark white underwear. A tent started to form in Gabe's shorts. She took off her bra and panties, threw them in Gabe's face, then jumped into the water, splashing and giggling.

Two minutes later, Gabe's mother marched over to the lake and said, "Gabe Arthur Chaplin, you get your butt out of the water and your clothes on, because you're coming home with me right now!" Martha sounded like a bull horn at a sporting event. Gabe spun around, splashing Mary as he did.

"I thought you said your mother wasn't home." Mary turned around, so that her back was facing Gabe's mother.

"She wasn't supposed to be," Gabe said, feeling about as tall as a blade of grass. He shook his head and looked away.

Martha stood at the foot of the lake. She had taken her shoes off and was holding them.

"I see you out there, Mary Esher." Martha had put her hand over her eyes to cut down the shimmering glare from the moon.

"My parents are gonna kill me," Mary said.

"Don't you dare bring up her name," Gabe said now. "Do you know how much pain and suffering you caused me for years because of what you did? So don't you dare go and tell me that that night was my fault. Do you hear me?" Gabe locked his eyes on his mother and clenched his fists.

He hurried into the kitchen, now at the boiling point, and got some milk from the refrigerator. He peeked over his shoulder only to see his mother hobbling in. She moved with the speed of a snail, and grunted and moaned like a wounded animal. Gabe often worried that if a fire broke out and she was alone, she'd never be able to get out in time. Martha used to get around with a walker, but had tripped over it so many times that she had finally thrown it down the cellar stairs out of frustration. She now walked with a cane which had three rubber knobs on the end when she needed to. At times, when she went into one of her violent rages, she would use the thing to knock over dishes, glasses, whatever she could hit.

"Don't you go and blame that night on *me*. You were the one who went out there, swimming with that girl in the nude. In case you've forgotten, you were only seventeen back then."

"You've got to be kidding. How could I have forgotten? I could never forget that night!"

Gabe slammed the refrigerator door, rattling the bottles inside. He then stormed past his mother with a glass of milk in his hand.

"Get back in here."

Martha followed him.

Gabe sat down on the couch and picked up the remote control. He put his feet up, sipped his milk, and surfed through the channels. Martha cared about one thing in the world and that was her television. She'd watch the thing twenty-four hours a day if she could. She finally inched into the living room, cane and all.

"How many times do I have to tell you not to change the channels so fast? If you break my TV, you're going to have to buy me another one. And both of us know *you* can't afford to."

"Well maybe if you helped pay for some of my college expenses, I might have some money," he snapped back, and continued to flip through the channels.

Martha stood in front of the television. For a few long seconds, she didn't say a word. She just glared at him like some angry guard dog about to attack. Gabe could only see a fraction of the screen, but he still surfed through the channels.

"I told you to stop switching the channels like that! You're going to break the clicker!"

Gabe threw the remote down and rose.

"Hey, I'm not finished with you. Get back here!" Martha moved slightly away from the television and in Gabe's direction.

Gabe turned and looked at his mother. If he left now, she would storm into his room in the middle of the night to badger him some more.

"If I could help you with your college expenses, I would." Gabe looked at her as if he didn't recognize her. "When all is said and done, I'm going to leave the house to you." Tears poured from her eyes.

Gabe walked over and held her like a baby. She put her head on his shoulder and cried.

"Oh, look what I've gone and done," Martha said, pulling away from his soaked shirt. "Let me get a tissue." She wiped her eyes with the back of her hand.

"Don't worry about it, Mother. I'll be fine." Gabe looked at her through his own blurred eyes.

CHAPTER THREE

A week passed before Gabe saw Sara again. He stopped by the museum every chance he could, but she wasn't there. He even asked one of the employees for her address, but the museum did not give out any personal information on its employees. He would have looked her number up in the phone book, but he didn't know her last name. He didn't think she lived too far, considering that she rode her bike to work. But where?

It was just after one o'clock in the afternoon, and Gabe was on his way out of the museum, when a hand gripped his shoulder. He turned, and his eyes locked on a towering figure that made him shiver.

"I was wondering if you've happened to have seen that girl who works here—you know, the one with the special ability to change her appearance?" The tall man smiled, his piercing, glowing, stormy-blue, close-set eyes stared.

"Excuse me?" Gabe gazed back.

"Why don't we go for a walk? I have something to tell you that I believe you'll find quite interesting." The tall man started down the steep steps. He turned and looked up. "Well, are you coming?"

For a brief moment, Gabe didn't know what to do—he was intrigued, but, at the same time, distrustful. His curiosity won out. He nodded and followed.

The tall man rubbed his hands together. "I bet you really like her, don't you."

"Who, Sara?"

"Is that her name now? You don't know how hard it is to keep up with her. I guess that's what happens when you get old like myself. Listen, I don't have a lot of time to fill in all the details, but I'll start by saying her history is old as the Crucifixion. And unlike her, it's not pretty."

Gabe stopped. "Now, wait a second. I have no idea what you're talking about. I hardly know her. We only met a week ago. And if you haven't noticed, she's only a teenager."

The tall man's bushy gray eyebrows rose. "Now, that's a good one." He leaned over and pointed a long bony finger at Gabe. "You listen to me. If you stay with her you'll lose your soul like so many others have."

Gabe's eyes widened. "Now I recognize you! You were in the museum when I met her!"

The tall man smiled, displaying a mouthful of yellow crooked teeth. "I've seen her do that too many times to count. Don't be fooled by her charm. She may look like any normal teenager, but she's anything but. Stay away from her, or you'll lose yourself. Just stay away from her." He turned and walked back up the stairs.

"But wait, you can't say all that and just leave. I've got questions." The tall man ignored him and continued walking up the stairs. Gabe shook his head, walked back to his car wondering what the hell was going on, and then headed for class.

###

Three hours later, Gabe's advanced-painting class had just ended. He zipped out of the classroom with his paint box and latest canvas so fast that he accidentally slammed it against the door frame.

Outside, a bright spring day greeted him. Sparrows and blue jays were building nests and singing tunes that only they knew. In his haste, Gabe missed their songs.

Gabe blew one red light, a stop sign, and arrived at 4:20. He looked for Sara's bike, but it wasn't on the bicycle rack. He didn't know what hours she worked, or if she was working at all, so he sat in his car and waited. He flipped on the radio and listened to the only rock station one could get in Southwick, WSRW, and on a good day it faded in and out like short wave. The excitement and crowds the museum created when it first opened was starting to die down. The parking lot wasn't even half full. Looking at his watch only made time pass more slowly. Restless, he got out of the car and walked over to the bicycle rack to have another look. He tried desperately to spot Sara's, but it wasn't there. Dejected, he kicked at the ground, sending a cloud of dust drifting. When he headed back to his car, he heard a swishing sound. He saw someone on a bike heading his way. He squinted but still couldn't make out who was on the bike. That didn't stop his heart from thumping, or the rush of adrenaline he felt tingling in his veins.

The first feature he saw was black hair flowing as the person pedaled toward him. When he saw Sara's face, his heart raced faster. He cupped his hand over his mouth and shouted, "Sara!"

She turned and said, "Gabe, is that you?" She stopped pedaling and walked the bike to the rack. Gabe hurried over to meet her. He couldn't wait to kiss her.

"Where have you been?" he asked.

Sara shielded her eyes from the sun and said, "Why don't we sit over there." She pointed to the shade a large maple was providing. "Just let me first lock up my bike. This is my only means of transportation."

Side by side, they walked over to the maple tree, which stood like some long-forgotten guardian, its branches spread out like a thousand hands. They sat in the cool shade.

"Where have you been?" Gabe asked again, not taking an eye off of her.

"I've been home, sick in bed."

"Sick? Well, whatever you had you sure don't look to have it now."

Sara smiled. "I had a bad stomach. The doctor said that the shock, or guilt, as he likes to call it, over the deaths of my mother and sister, brings this out in me every so often. I haven't been the same since."

"I'm sorry to hear that." He paused. "Listen, I don't know how to say this, but I spoke with a man earlier today and he had some pretty weird things to say about you. I thought he was just nuts, but when I thought back to what happened to your face the day we met, he didn't sound so crazy."

Sara blushed and shook her head, and rose. "What do you mean?"

Gabe shrugged. "Your face. It changed. Your hair was stringy and brown, and your skin was dark like you lay out in the sun all summer long."

She gazed. "You really saw that?"

Gabe shook his head. "Yes, I did."

"Was the man you spoke with real tall?"

"Tall as a stallion."

"What about his eyes?"

"They were the most intense I've ever seen."

Sara rubbed her forehead and took a few deep breaths. She staggered. Gabe reached for her and said, "Are you okay?"

She put out her hand and said, "I'll be fine. Just give me a few seconds." She took a few more deep breaths. "It's not every day the man from your dreams comes to life."

"So that's what you were talking about in the bathroom. I thought you were speaking to someone."

"No, just myself. I do it all the time." Sara cracked a smile, and pushed her hair out of her face, but the wind kept blowing it back. "I've tried to tell my family about what I sometimes see staring back at me in the mirror, but since they haven't seen my face transform yet, they just think I'm nuts. But I can't be now that you've seen it."

"But how can your face change like that?"

She shrugged. "I wish I could tell you, but I haven't a clue."

"I don't know what it means either but I know it has to do with the tall man. If anyone has the answers he does," Gabe said.

"Have you ever had a thought right at the tip of your tongue and forgot what it was?"

Gabe nodded.

"Well that's what the tall man is to me." She paused. "You know, I live with my father, younger sister Jenna, grandmother, and grandfather. Let's just say it's quite interesting having all those different age groups under one roof. My grandmother Winnie is so cool. She tells such fascinating stories that you wish she'd never stop. She could keep an audience of a thousand spellbound with any one of her stories." Sara smiled.

Gabe could see she didn't want to talk any more about her face transforming or the tall man, so he let it be. "That sounds great. I never had the chance to know my grandparents. They all died before I was born, though I did hear some things about them. My great-great-great-grandfather was in the Civil War. He was quite a photographer in his time. I've got pictures of him hanging in my room. I framed them real nice, too."

"I'd love to have a look at them some day. You told me that you've been taking care of your sick mother. That must be hard on you."

Gabe rolled his eyes. "It sure is. She's been sick for years. She's been to quite a few doctors, and none of them can tell what's wrong with her. Some have even said it's all just in her head, and sometimes I tend to agree with them. Though she is in a deep depression, but that shouldn't pardon her for the way she treats me." Gabe shook his head.

"What about your family? Can't they help take care of her?"

"Family! I wouldn't know a family if they were sitting next to me." Gabe stood and looked away. He kicked at a stone and missed it. "My mother and I live alone."

Sara walked toward him. "I'm sorry to hear that. I guess I take having a family for granted."

"You don't have to be sorry." He turned and looked her in the eyes. For an instant, time stood still. Caught in her stare, Gabe moved closer, his stomach aflame. Their lips pressed together in a passionate embrace. He wanted it to never end. After a while, they slowly pulled away. Gabe felt like he had been pulled off his feet by a gust of wind and had flown through the sky like a bird.

"I hope you don't mind what just happened." Gabe nervously kicked at the ground.

Sara's eyes fluttered. "Mind, you've got to be kidding. I just had the best kiss of my life. And I've had a few," she said with a smile, and then glanced at her watch. "I've gotta get inside. I'm already late, but believe me, I'd stay here with you all day if I could."

She reached into her pants' pocket for a pen. "Do you have something I can write on? I want to give you my number and address. I don't know about you, but this past week of not seeing or hearing from you was a killer. I didn't even know your last name to look up your number."

Gabe smiled pleased to know that she had missed him as much as he had her, pulled out a piece of paper from his front pants' pocket, and handed it to her. "Here, this is all I've got."

Using her palm for a desk, Sara wrote down her full name, phone number, and where she lived. "Here you go," she said with a smile and handed it back to him.

"Sara Livingston. That's a beautiful name." Sara blushed. "You live off of Route 58?"

"That's right." She again pushed the hair out of her face. "I live just down the block from the shooting range."

"How do you sleep at night?" Gabe laughed.

"You get used to it. Well, I'd better get going now."

He ripped the piece of paper in half and scribbled down his own information. "Here. You'd better not forget this." He handed her the ripped piece of paper and then kissed her again. She ran toward the museum. She looked back and smiled again just before she walked inside.

Gabe smiled and kicked up his heels. For the time being, he had forgotten about the situation with his mother. Suddenly he saw the crows sitting lifeless in an oak tree. Their black feathers looked like leaves since the tree had only small buds that had just begun to spurt. The birds were as silent as an empty classroom. Gabe looked up at them and then back at the museum. "What is it with these birds?" He shook his head and looked at them again.

CHAPTER FOUR

Loaded down with art supplies, Gabe tiptoed into the house. Then it dawned on him that Mrs. Brown was coming over to see his mother. A glance at the clock on the wall told him that Mrs. Brown would be at the door in less than forty-five minutes. He quickly started cleaning the front door window but realized after five minutes that he'd never have the time to finish the whole house. He concentrated on the kitchen first, which was the dirtiest, and then the living room.

The kitchen was as run-down as the rest of the house. The brick-colored plastic tile floor had wear marks in front of the stove, which worked when it wanted to, and the sink. The microwave made a loud popping sound when it was set to high, not to mention the smell it emitted which was similar to the stench of burning plastic. The refrigerator leaked so much water that every few days it had to be mopped up, and as for the dishwasher, it hadn't seen a dish in years and was caked inside with green mold.

Twenty minutes later, he was finished. He took the vacuum out of the kitchen closet and started on the living room.

"Could you vacuum some other time. I'm trying to watch the TV," Martha yelled.

Gabe looked up and shook his head. "You'd think you'd keep

your mouth shut and let me do a good job. Besides, when aren't you watching TV?" he muttered under his breath. He moved the vacuum back and forth on a carpet so worn that in some spots the wooden floor showed through.

He continued to rush around, trying to get the house in some kind of order, and he still had to tell his mother what was going on. He'd just as soon face a tank full of flesh-eating fish.

Gabe had finished cleaning the living room and had just sat down in the kitchen when he heard the television go off and then his mother's heavy footsteps.

"What's going on?" Martha asked as she poked her head in the kitchen. "I haven't seen you move this fast in years. You look like you have ants in your pants. Remember when that happened to you and Eddie Katz when you were eight years old?" Martha smiled.

He got up and shook his head in annoyance. "I have something to tell you. Why don't you have a seat." He did not want to relive a past that at times felt like an open wound.

Martha inched her way over to the kitchen table.

Gabe tried to help his mother sit down, but she pushed him away. "I can handle it," she snapped. "Now, what is it that you have to tell me?" She picked up a napkin and blew her nose until every bit of snot was free. Then she wiped it clean like a baby's behind.

"Would you please stop that? You know how much I hate the trumpeting sound your nose makes. Would you like something to drink?" Anything to avoid what he had to tell her.

She shook her head and tapped her fingers on the table. "If I wanted something to drink I would've already asked you. Now could we please get on with this! I've got my shows to watch."

He prepared for the worst-case scenario—his mother going through the roof. He looked her straight in the eyes and said, "Listen, Mother, a friend is coming over to see you today."

She laughed. "A friend? What are you talking about? I have no friends."

"She's not your friend, she's a friend of mine. What I'm trying to say is—"

"Now just spit it out."

"I saw Mrs. Brown at the museum last week. She's a therapist who works at the Taylor Institute. I asked her to come over and talk with you." His deep breath came out in a whoosh.

"The Taylor Institute!" Martha exclaimed with such force that the roof to their house nearly lifted up a few inches. "That's a loony bin—a place for crazy people! You're not taking me there, not for a second are you!" She pointed a finger at him as her face contorted into a river of deep depressions and ridges.

"Whoever said I was taking you anywhere?"

"Don't kid with me, Gabe. I know all they need is a signature and I'm off with the guys in the white coats. You wouldn't do that to your own mother, would you?" Her brownish-gray eyebrows rose.

"I'm not sending you anywhere, Mother. So just sit back and listen, and I don't want to hear another word out of you. Do we understand each other?" She folded her hands and placed them on the table. They looked weathered and old like she made a living on the sea. "Mrs. Brown is a real nice lady. She's just going to ask you some questions, and all you have to do is answer them. That's all, and it will be over sooner than you know."

"What's it gonna cost?"

"Mother, I'm sure your insurance will cover it." Gabe sighed.

"They'd better, or you can forget about it."

"I've got to take a shower. Can I trust you in here alone?"

"Of course you can," she said with a devilish grin.

The house was silent except for the persistent sound of water dripping in the kitchen sink—drip, drip, drip, like the beat to a song.

Gabe showered in four minutes flat, put on a white cotton shirt, a pair of stonewashed jeans, and rushed out of the bathroom holding his sneakers and socks. He heard the TV playing, but that didn't matter—he still wanted to see his mother and make sure everything was okay. He could not remember the last time she had left the house, but if she was ever going to, this would be the time.

Standing at the edge of the living room carpet, Gabe saw the back of her head as she sat crocheting in front of the television.

"Mother, why don't you sell those things. We already have enough to last a lifetime." Gabe sat on the floor and slipped on his socks and sneakers.

His mother continued to watch the television and crochet like a machine.

"You'd better hope Mrs. Brown gets here soon. *Oprah* is coming on in an hour, and you know I can't miss her." She watched the show twice a day, catching the reruns on the local cable station at night. She taped them too, just in case she wanted to watch *Oprah* on weekends, or late at night when the show wasn't on.

Gabe headed back to the bathroom to blow dry his hair, which he rarely did, and fix himself up for Mrs. Brown. Gabe was nervous and didn't know what to expect—especially from his mother.

Ten minutes later, Gabe sat in the kitchen, finishing a glass of milk and cookies when he heard a knock on the door. "I'll get it, Mother." He quickly wiped his lips and placed the glass in the sink.

Gabe flew out of the kitchen to answer the door, and there was Mrs. Brown. The middle-aged woman wore a long, royal blue skirt that hung just above her black leather shoes that had sparkling gold buckles. She wore a pair of red designer glasses that looked too big for her face, her lips were painted in a pastel rose-colored lipstick, and her eye shadow was a light brown. A far cry from how she looked last week at the museum opening, when she wore no makeup, and had on a pair of jeans.

"Nice to see you again, Arthur," Mrs. Brown plainly said as she stood there holding a fashionable black leather case under her arm.

"Why don't you come in and have a seat. That's my mother over there on the couch."

The television was so loud you could barely hear yourself think. Gabe walked over to his mother and quietly asked her to turn off the television, but she waved him away. Gabe took the remote off the coffee table and did it himself. He then put the remote in his back pocket. Emily looked with raised eyebrows. The tension between Gabe and his mother was palpable, like a tight rope about to snap.

"You can leave the television on. Just lower the volume so we can talk. Do you mind if I sit down? I've been on my feet all day," Emily said.

"Oh, sure. Please have a seat," Gabe said, giving his mother a dirty look. He switched the television on and lowered the volume.

Emily sat in the black leather recliner, which was by far the best seat in the house, mainly because nobody ever used it. Martha preferred to sit in the same spot she'd been sitting for the past six years—the left side of the couch. It was so worn that her body fit as if the two were molded for each other.

Emily took out a yellow legal pad and a silver pen, folded one leg over the other, and fixed her skirt. "Mrs. Chaplin, I'm here today so that we can get to know each other a little bit. If you're not up to answering any of the questions I'm about to ask, please let me know and I'll go on to another. Or, if you want, we can just talk about whatever you'd like."

Emily was about the most soft-spoken person Gabe had ever met.

"How are you feeling today, Mrs. Chaplin?"

Martha slightly rocked back and forth before she answered. Emily noted this on her pad. "I guess I feel all right today, or at least no worse than I do on most days. You see, I don't move around that much and my limbs become tight and sore, so that it becomes too painful to even walk," Martha said as she continued to rock. Gabe watched as Emily wrote and underlined the words "no worse" in her pad.

"What do you suppose you could do to ease the pain you're feeling?" Emily pushed her glasses up with the tip of her index finger.

"Dr. Roberts prescribed these pills for me," Martha said, reaching for the bottle on the coffee table. "But they make me sick to my stomach and tired. Right, Gabe?" Martha looked over at him, and Gabe nodded.

"That's right, Mom." He still didn't know what to think of all of this. He had never gone to a counselor, other than his high school one.

"Do you mind if I take a look at those pills?" Emily pointed to the coffee table.

"Sure, go ahead," Martha said.

Emily picked up the bottle and copied down the name of the prescription. "How long have you been taking Valium?"

"Ever since I had my second breakdown three and a half years ago."

Gabe looked away. He hated being reminded of the past.

After a few more questions, Emily stopped. Gabe was influencing his mother's answers—every time Emily asked a question, Martha would look over to Gabe and then answer it.

Emily put down her pen and pad. "Would you mind if we take a break, Mrs. Chaplin?"

"Sure, why not. If you like, Gabe could get us something to drink."

"You know, I could go for a cup of tea. Why don't I join you in the kitchen," Emily said to Gabe. She got up and followed him.

He reached into the cupboard and pulled out a metal tin that had originally been filled with cookies from last Christmas. "There's tea bags, sugar, and Sweet and Low in the tin. If you want coffee, we only have instant." Gabe took milk from the refrigerator, placed it on the counter, and then checked the kettle on the stove. There was enough water in it, so he turned it on.

"Tea will be fine. Gabe, it must be difficult having to take care of your mother all by yourself." She took two sugars from the tin, along with one tea bag.

Gabe reached into another cupboard and pulled out two plain white mugs. He gave one to Emily and placed the other on the counter for his mother. "Yes, at times it can be difficult. I'm twenty years old, and I'm a prisoner in my own home, and with college, my time is already limited. Do you know how much I have to give up to take care of my mother? It doesn't seem fair."

Emily sat down at the kitchen table. "I'd say you've done a heck of a job, considering the circumstance, but you need to live too. Have you talked about this with your mother?"

Gabe sighed. "I've tried to, but she doesn't want to hear it. It's kind of like I'm programmed to be just what she wants me to be. Don't get me wrong—we have plenty of arguments, but they don't really get us anywhere. They only seem to fuel the fire." Gabe sat down with his emotions on the table.

"Why don't you let me talk to your mother alone. I think she'll open up more if you're not with us. Do you have something to do?" Emily asked as the kettle started whistling.

Gabe walked over to the stove and turned off the fire, but he couldn't turn off the one that was burning inside. He walked back to the table and poured the water for Emily's and his mother's tea. "I can leave the house, if that's what you want me to do," Gabe snapped.

Emily plopped in a tea bag, stirred in the sugar, and added a drop of milk. Gabe made his mother's tea, making sure to add the ice.

"You take care of my mother, and please let me know what's going on. If it was up to her, I'm sure she wouldn't tell a soul, including me."

"Of course, you'll know exactly what's going on with her."

Gabe picked up his mother's cup, and was about to bring it to her, but Emily put out her hand. "I'll take it."

For the first time in his life, Gabe felt useless in his own home. Soon Emily would know everything, and from his mother's perspective, which bothered him.

He rushed out the side door, hopped into his car, and skidded out of the driveway. He drove around town and headed down Route 58. In long stretches it was barren with old, abandoned farmhouses, broken fences, windmills, and barns on either side. Gabe pulled over with a screech and parked the car. Rays of sunlight shone through the car window and warmed his arm. Not a cloud was out. He placed his folded arms on the steering wheel and rested his head on them. He inhaled the smell of wild grass as it swayed in the breeze. Even though he had approached Mrs. Brown about speaking to his mother, he now had second thoughts. The bag was now open, and soon all the goodies would be on display. On many occasions, he wished his mother dead, but now he felt guilty about the way he'd been treating her. After a few minutes alone with his thoughts, Gabe started the car and drove all the way to the end of Route 58, turned around, and headed back.

He returned home twenty minutes later. Emily's green Explorer was no longer parked out in the street.

"At least she's not here," he said, and headed for his house, not knowing what to expect from his mother.

He came through the front door, slamming it hard. He wanted to make sure she knew he was home, but there wasn't a sound in the house. Even the television was off. Gabe looked in the kitchen and then went to his mother's room. He banged hard on the door. Wincing and shaking his hand, he listened for running water but heard nothing. He checked the bathroom, and it too was empty. He headed for the basement. He opened the door, which squeaked like an old bearing, and looked downstairs, his stomach tightening. His mother had tripped numerous times on these stairs in the past; the last accident occurred six months ago—the two had argued over the use of the television. Gabe had wanted to watch a program on the arts, but *Oprah* was on, and his mother wouldn't miss the show for anything. He had been furious that night. He even tried to explain to her that the VCR could tape one channel while you're watching another. But she didn't want to hear a thing. As she was fond of saying, *Your mother and technology are on opposite ends of the earth.* The TV and VCR were off limits to anyone but her. But Gabe had pushed the issue that day and finally did get to watch the program he wanted to, but in the process, his mother had gone downstairs to try the old black-and-white TV and had nearly killed herself walking back up.

The basement was now dark, but he still wanted to have a look. He envisioned his mother lying on the floor at the bottom of the steps, all twisted, bent, and her neck broken. But the only thing he found was the same junk that had been there since he was a kid. But on the way up, he noticed a stained brown box on the shelf against the wall, poking out as if someone had looked through it. He carefully carried the box over to a Ping-Pong table that was littered with old clothes and other boxes covered in dust, and Christmas stuff that should have been put away months ago. He pulled the string to the light that hung above the table. The windows were so dirty that hardly any light from outside could get in. He dusted off the box and opened it to have a look. The box was filled with opened letters and mostly old black-and-white photographs of landscapes he knew weren't from the USA. He remembered that his father had been in the Korean War and had been stationed in Germany for some time. Those were times Gabe knew little about. After the divorce, his mother never did talk much about those days. It seemed anything connected with that time was off limits. He continued to dig through the musty box and found a thick tan envelope folded in half and wrapped in rubber bands that had dried out and stuck together. Gabe pulled them off and opened the envelope. He took out what looked to be documents bound with staples at the top. He read the beginning of the first page and saw the name and address of a law firm in town, and below that, his parents' names in bold text.

"This must be my parents' divorce papers." Still reading them, Gabe walked to the edge of the steps and sat down.

Five minutes later, he came upon something he would have never liked to have read. He looked up and stared.

"He used to beat her. But how could I have forgotten?" Gabe shook his head. "But I swear I don't remember."

Gabe put everything back, returned the box to where he had found it, and headed back upstairs, shaking his head.

Standing in the kitchen, he heard two car doors slam and then his mother's voice, which he knew like a record played over and over—she had a thin nasal one, and when she yelled, it became heavy like bass. Gabe couldn't remember the last time his mother had stepped out of the house, other than to go in the back yard to grow her flowers when she was able to. He quickly headed back downstairs, stopping at the second step from the top, and left the door open just enough so he could listen and see.

"You can call me tomorrow between nine in the morning and twelve noon. After that, I'll be on the road, but you can beep me.

My beeper number is just below my work number," Emily said, handing Martha her business card.

"Wait. Before you go, would you please be kind enough to explain what a beeper is? Because I haven't a clue," Martha said. She sat down on the couch.

"You're putting me on, right?" Emily said.

Martha's brow creased as she looked at the business card. Gabe snickered to himself.

Emily walked over to where Martha sat and unclipped her beeper from the strap on her leather bag. "All you have to do is dial my beeper number on your phone. Wait for a beeping sound, then punch in your own number on the phone, and this black box will beep and show me your number in the little window. Do you understand the principle?" she asked.

"I think so. Let's just hope I don't have to beep you," Martha said with a smile.

"Good enough. Now you take care and remember what I said." Emily gave Martha's arm a squeeze and then left.

Only one line gained Gabe's interest, and that was the last one. He heard the front door close, then quickly rushed through the kitchen and into the living room. His mother had already switched on the television.

"So how'd it go?" he asked, and sat down next to her.

"You'll never guess what I did." Martha turned down the volume on the TV, which was something she rarely did.

"I'm all ears."

"I took a ride with Mrs. Brown. She drove me to Wildwood Park. I was all nerves the whole way there." Martha raised her hands and smiled.

"I bet you were," Gabe said, trying his best to sound interested.

"We talked about a lot of things. I just opened up like a happy clam. You should have seen me!" Martha paused for a moment to glance at the television. "She wants me to have a full exam with another doctor. When I told her whom I was seeing, she nearly fell out of her seat. She's also prescribing a new drug for me. I think it's called Zoltar or Zoloft. Whatever it is, she says it should help me, unlike what I've been taking for so long. In a very nice way she told me my doctor was off his rocker, and was more concerned with how much money he could milk from my insurance company than finding out what's wrong with me. And to think, I trusted the man all these years." She shook her head.

Gabe took a deep breath and listened to his mother speak as she had never done before. He couldn't believe the change he saw before his eyes. For the first time in a long while, he saw his mother as another person, and it scared him.

"When you first told me about Mrs. Brown I cringed, but now I feel differently," his mother said with a smile. And smiling wasn't something he saw her do all that much.

They conversed for a while longer, with his mother doing most of the talking. Gabe was tongue-tied but managed to say, "I've heard people speak of miracles, and I've never believed in them myself, but after seeing the change in you today, I guess anything is possible." Gabe frowned—he suddenly felt overwhelmed as he thought about his mother's sudden transformation and the documents he had found downstairs.

"Thanks, Gabe, but I have to tell you, I'm scared stiff of what's going to happen next. I've lived a certain way for such a long time— so change isn't going to come easy. Emily told me I'm just like a child now—learning all over again. I hope you can bear with me."

CHAPTER FIVE

Three weeks had passed since Gabe's mother had first seen Emily Brown. Martha had seen her three times since then and had steadily progressed with each passing day. Her new prescription seemed to be helping too. Gabe still couldn't believe what was happening—his mother looked different, talked different, did everything different, but one thing still remained—her watching the television. She didn't watch it as much, but it still was very much a big part of her life.

The drive to the therapist's office was a quiet one until Gabe broached the subject that had been on his mind since he had discovered the divorce papers.

"Mom, I don't know how to say this, but a few weeks ago I found a box out of place on the shelf downstairs. I—"

"What did I tell you about snooping into things that aren't yours? How many—"

"Now don't you go and give me that. Someone had already taken the box down, and I know it wasn't you. It had to have been Emily. Why didn't you ever tell me about what Dad did to you?" Gabe shook his head.

"Because I felt you already had enough problems in a house without a father."

"But I don't remember him ever beating you."

"He was out of the house by the time you were five years old. Thank God for that. There's no telling what he would have done."

Gabe looked out the window and felt a twinge in the back of his head. He slowly turned and looked at his mother. "Did he ever beat me?"

Their eyes locked, and then she looked away.

"I said, did he ever beat me?" Gabe asked as the pain in his head grew to a slow throb.

His mother turned back with tears in her eyes and said, "I'm afraid he did."

"You should have told me, Mother. What other things have you kept from me over the years?"

She just cried into her hands. He almost did himself.

Ten minutes later, he parked in front of the professional building. He helped his mother out of the car. She now walked without her cane but still needed aid over rough terrain. Gabe walked her into the office.

"Okay, Mother. I'll be back at the therapist's around three thirty to pick you up." He kissed her on the cheek and then headed back to his car. He opened the window halfway and drove to Sara's house, wondering how much more he didn't know about his family.

The sun shone like a piece of hot coal, and the breeze tickled his face. Pine trees were green and full, and the fresh scent they emitted helped to lift his mood. Poplars' still skeletons were starting to bud, and little green strands of grass as fine as baby's hair were starting to poke their way through the dark rich soil. Soon, life in Southwick would again be in full bloom. After one of the coldest winters in its history, Gabe was overjoyed with the sight of spring just around the corner. After the last frost, crops would soon be planted and then harvested for the wave of summer people traveling and vacationing.

Gabe enjoyed the rush of cool air as it hit him in the face. His hair was everywhere. With this being his first visit to Sara's house, the wind on his face helped to calm his nerves. He flipped on the radio and found a good rocker, the Stones' "Paint It Black." He tapped the steering wheel in perfect time as the song played out. He sang along too, but not in that patented Jagger voice.

He passed the shooting range and made his first left, which was Wild Neck Road. Sara lived in house no. 226. Wild Neck had more twists and turns than a roller coaster ride. Generations of teenagers, including Gabe, had enjoyed joyriding on the road and playing mailbox baseball. He looked for the landmark Sara had given him—a broken-down windmill.

Gabe gripped the wheel. The urge to pull over and have a look filled his body like cold fright. He parked the car and slowly walked over to it. The windmill looked small from the roadside, but when he stood a few feet in front of it, he realized it measured well over three stories high. Gabe looked up and was blinded by the sun. He lowered his gaze, blinking, and walked toward the hulking vane. One of the runners had fallen to the ground and still lay there half buried in the dirt; the others had rotted down to their wooden frames. Tatters of a ripped sheet flapped in the strengthening breeze. The windmill looked surreal, standing there all by itself in the middle of a vacant field with tall wild grass swishing back and forth from an overpowering wind that pushed Gabe toward the entrance of the mill. The door gaped open with jagged splinters of wood that had an uncanny resemblance to teeth in a rotted skull.

Inside, it was nearly pitch dark except for streams of light that filtered in through fallen boards and cracks, to create ragged patterns on the walls and floor. Gabe hesitantly walked along, jumping in surprise as glass crunched underfoot. He glanced down; empty beer bottles, many of them broken, and cigarette butts, littered the ground. He paused at the ruffle of feathers and a faint crowing from above. He looked up, trying to pierce the blackness that cloaked the rafters, but all he saw was the occasional flash of something moving.

A shadow danced on the wall opposite him. He looked over his shoulder and spied a figure moving toward him. His palms were moist. His throat went dry, and his heart thumped. He turned and headed for the doorway, but his foot turned on a rock, and he fell against the wall. The thud startled whatever hid in the rafters—the sound of crowing and feathers ruffling grew in volume. To his amazement, the birds didn't come after him but rather, they flew out of the mill and circled high above.

He tried to scream, but nothing came out. He pushed away from the wall and ran as fast as he could toward his car. Once inside, he locked the doors and rolled up the windows, and only then did he look back. The birds were now only specks in the sky as they flew high above the mill. He saw a tall figure standing there as still as a scarecrow. He blinked twice, and the figure was gone.

Five minutes later, Gabe pulled into Sara's driveway and parked behind an old Ford pickup—he had just managed to get his breath back. She lived in a Victorian farmhouse. It had three stories and a screened-in porch that ran three quarters of the way around. The house bore fresh-looking lemon yellow paint. The roof was black like licorice, and the shutters were a deep forest green. Gabe saw the steel gray storm cellar doors open and could hear his mother telling him about the great storm of 1959.

Gabe spotted Sara at the front door. He got out of the car and met her halfway up the driveway. Sara was all smiles. "I'm glad you could make it. It's so nice to see you."

Gabe sighed. He wanted to reach out and kiss her, but he saw a face looking from behind the screen door that led into her house.

"You look beautiful, Sara."

She smiled and her eyes fluttered. "You think so?" she said, and twirled around to show all sides. "I spent all morning trying on everything in my closet. And the funny thing about it was I went with the first thing I tried on. I just love the color purple." He looked at the purple sweater she wore, which was fuzzy like a cat's locks.

"You know, some day I'm going to have to paint you."

Sara blushed. "You really mean that?"

"Of course I do."

"Let's go inside. I want to introduce you to my family. They're dying to meet you." She put her arm around Gabe's waist and playfully pushed him along.

Now Gabe's stomach churned, and his back was wet with sweat. He followed Sara into her house and couldn't help but notice all the flowerbeds they passed. The flowers were still just green sprouts popping out of the dirt, but he imagined that in time they'd have petals in various shades. Gabe thought back to the last time his house had such flowers, and that was years ago when his mother used to plant—before she had gotten sick. Standing inside Sara's house, Gabe was introduced to her nine-year-old sister, Jenna, who had curly red hair, green eyes, and a round face that looked like a doll's.

"This is my sister, Jenna. Jenna, this is Gabe."

"Nice to meet you," Gabe said.

Jenna laughed and said, "So this is the boy you talk so much about." She then ran out of the house, laughing some more.

"You'll have to forgive her; she acts this way when she first meets someone. She's just trying to shock you," Sara said, cheeks flushed, as the front screen door slammed.

"She's doing a pretty good job." He smiled.

"We'll meet the rest of my family later. They stepped out for a few things at the supermarket. Would you like something to drink? Or how about a slice of blueberry pie? I made it myself."

"Sounds great."

They walked through a small hallway lined with photographs. Gabe could tell that most of them were old because of the sepia tone to them and their crinkled edges. Inside the kitchen, Gabe sat down on a tall swiveled bar stool. "I don't mean to stare, but this is the biggest kitchen I've ever seen."

"You think so?" She paused and looked. "It *is* big, isn't it," she said. She took the pie out of the refrigerator. "Would you like some milk with that, and how about a scoop of vanilla ice-cream on top?"

"The ice-cream sounds great, but I'll pass on the milk," Gabe said as he continued to look around in wonderment.

He saw a set of sliding doors just past the end of the counter top, and beyond that a wooden deck with waist-high walls. Looking out the sliders, he could see a back yard that seemed to stretch for miles.

"Do you own all that land back there?"

Sara shook her head. "No, not all of it." She cut two slices of pie. "You see that wooden shed on the left-hand side?"

"Yeah," Gabe said, seeing half of it.

"Well, just beyond that shed is a small metal fence made of chicken wire. That's our property line."

"Wow." His eyes widened. Either way, the yard was still large.

"Here you go. I hope you like it. They're last year's berries that we freeze so that we can use them all year long." Gabe took a plate and spoon from Sara and thanked her. "We can sit outside if you like," she said and looked toward the sliders.

"Sure, why not. It's a beautiful day." Gabe followed her.

The sun shone bright as a raging fire. Gabe sat down on a bench built into the wooden deck. Tied to the seat, long thick soft cushions, decorated in tight patterns of sunflowers, adorned the bench.

"This is the best blueberry pie I've ever tasted, and I've had my share," he said, and took another spoonful. "In the middle of summer we go to the fair at Reeves Park where everyone comes with their family and friends. They have a pie contest for cooking as well as for eating. You should enter it. Last year, John Swift ate fifteen apple pies in record time, but I'll tell you another time what happened after that," he said and looked down at his pie with a twisted face.

Gabe left out the part about how John Swift had gotten his revenge on a town that had made fun of his weight ever since he was seven years old. On that sunny summer day he had thrown up on all the other contestants and had created quite a scene.

Gabe ate his last spoonful of pie, got up, and walked over to the edge of the deck. "What a view you have out here," he said, leaning on the rail. Soon cornfields tall and plentiful would fill the barren landscape.

"Yes, it is exquisite, isn't it," Sara said, and looked over at the window where she saw Winnie's creased and weathered face smiling. Gabe looked and smiled too.

"I saw that man from your dreams again. For some strange

reason I pulled over to the side of the road and walked over to the broken-down windmill on the way to your house. The place gave me the creeps." Gabe shivered.

"He gives me the creeps too. You know, I can't make heads or tails of him. It's like a dream that you forget over time. But I know his presence here means something. I just wish I knew what."

Gabe shook his head. "So do I."

"Come on, let me show you our barn. You'll never guess what's in it." She ran down the steps leading into the back yard. Gabe quickly followed.

Sara jumped and spun about. She practically jigged her way over to the barn. When they finally got there, she stopped at the front doors and turned around with her arms folded and her legs set wide apart. The wind blew her hair in her face, and she pushed it away. "You've got to guess what's in here or I'm not gonna let you see." She smiled.

"Do I have to get it right on the first try?"

"Well . . ." She paused. "We'll see, but you'd better say something fast."

Gabe rubbed his hands together and smiled. "You've got a three-headed pig in there you don't want anyone to see."

Her face twisted. "Nope."

"A space ship, right?"

Sara shook her head. "Wrong again. I don't know, Gabe. Maybe you're just not good at this kind of game." She started to walk away from the barn.

"Now wait just a minute. I'm not leaving until you let me see what's behind those doors," he said, pointing toward them. "I mean it. I'll stay here all night and sleep in your back yard if I have to," he added, trying to hold back laughter.

"I'll let you see on one condition," she whispered.

"And what's that?" Gabe whispered back.

"You have to kiss me," she said with wide eyes.

"What torture."

He walked over to her, feeling like each step he took were a hundred. His heart thumped. He stood in front of her, closed his

eyes, and waited to feel the warmth of her breath. Their lips softly
locked together, and he kissed her like a seasoned lover. Gabe heard
the snap of a branch and abruptly pulled away. He craned his
neck, looked at the bushes behind Sara, and then smiled.

"What was that?"

Gabe pointed to the bushes. "Your sister."

Sara spun around to see Jenna's ponytails bouncing as she
reached the back door to the house. "You'll have to forgive me, but
my sister likes to get into everyone's business." Sara turned back to
Gabe and shook her head.

He waved his hand. "That's okay. You know, I'd do anything
to kiss you. I've never felt that close to anyone in my life. It was
like for a moment we were one." He shook his head. "I hope you
know what I mean."

Sara walked up to Gabe and put her hand on his shoulder. "I
sure do." She looked him in the eyes and smiled. "Now how about
I show you what's in the barn." She pointed toward it. "Behind
these doors is my father's pride and joy. Well, at least it *was* many
years ago." The barn door squeaked as she opened it. A few sparrows
flew out with a soft ruffle. Gabe covered up, having had enough of
birds for one day—for any day, for that matter.

A musty smell crept out. Stacked against the walls were shovels,
brooms, and a snow blower with its engine cover on the dirt floor
next to it. A chainsaw wet with oil, and a John Deer lawn mower
were stored in the back, as well as fertilizer, grass seed, and a red
toolbox as tall as the tall man. In the middle of it all lay something
large and covered with a tarp.

"Well, this is it," she said as started to pull the canvas cover off.
"Could you give me a hand?" Gabe grabbed the dusty canvas and
pulled as hard as he could. Little specks of dust glittered in the
soft rays of broken sunlight.

"So what do you think?"

Gabe's eyebrows rose. "Now, that's a car." He moved around it
to see from every angle. "When I was a kid, I remember driving in
something just like this—big round wheel wells, wrap-around front
and back glass, big chrome bumpers, thick whitewall tires, and

more room than a bedroom. It's a Lincoln, right?" He continued to gaze at the car.

"A Lincoln it is," a rather deep voice said from behind. Gabe turned around to see a middle-aged man standing in the doorway with his hands behind his back. "Sara, what are you doing out here?" he asked as he strolled over toward the car.

"I was just showing Gabe your car. I hope you don't mind," she said, her eyes fluttering.

"She sure could use a helping hand. You know, I'm not half bad with body work," Gabe said, and walked over to Sara's father.

"Dad, this is Gabe. Gabe, this is my father." Gabe smiled and firmly shook hands with Johnny.

"So you like to do body work. What do you think about her?" he said, smiling.

"Well, I haven't looked too closely at it yet, but I'd say that with some work it could be fixed." Gabe studied the many rust spots, dents, scratches, and faded black paint. "Is it a 1951 Lincoln?"

"Close, it's a '56. I've been wanting to restore her for years now, but I never seem to have the time," Johnny said and eyed the car as if it were a beautiful woman.

"I guess I could help you."

"Really?"

Gabe saw Mr. Livingston and himself driving down Route 58 with the windows down, their hair blowing in the wind (what was left of Mr. Livingston's), and old rock and roll songs blasting through the speakers. He smiled.

"When can you start?" Johnny asked and finally pulled his attention from the car.

Gabe froze. "I . . . I guess Saturday would be the earliest."

"That's fine with me. Well, I'll let you two alone." Sara's father passed by both of them on his way back to the house.

"I've never seen my father so happy, Gabe. You two hit it off perfectly well. I'm glad I came out here and showed you his car."

Gabe shook his head and looked away.

"What's wrong?"

He leaned up against the car and rubbed his chin. "I think I just got myself into something I can't handle. I'm really not that good with cars, and the only bodywork I've done was on my first car, which has long since seen its death. Your father's car is a classic, and fully restored, could be worth a lot of money. I just wouldn't want to mess it up." Gabe kicked at the dirt.

"Enough of this. My father isn't that good at restoring cars either. I'm sure you saw that red pickup parked in the driveway out front," Sara said, pointing toward her house.

Gabe looked up. "I sure did."

"Well, that was the first car he tried to restore. I really think he just wants to work on it with someone. I'm sure he'll be glad to teach you what he knows, considering you've already whet his appetite."

"Could you talk to him about it? I'd really appreciate it."

"Sure. I'll talk to him after dinner tonight."

"Thanks," Gabe said, relieved. "Want to go for a ride? I know this really cool park out on the fork!"

"Sure, but let me tell my father first. He goes bananas when I don't tell him where I'm going. I'll be right back." She ran to the back of the house and disappeared through the back door.

Gabe felt as good as he ever had, but something loomed in the foreground of his mind: the tall man.

Gabe stood outside the barn, enjoying the view, as he waited for Sara. The sun was directly behind her house, with shadows sprawling everywhere in neat little pockets. Gabe found the effect fascinating—he had been trying to capture it in his paintings ever since he realized the way a light source affected real life. Gabe had often used this effect in his work. Just recently, he had done a painting of the quad at his college. The square had benches on all sides, trees and shrubs, a waterfall in the middle, and green leafy ivy that ran up the brick wall and around the windows. Everyone hung out there when the weather was nice, and on certain days when the sun shone just right, it created a pattern of dark shadows that almost looked surreal, like the shadows in a Dali painting. When Gabe had completed the painting and handed it in, he had won praise from many of his professors and just about everyone who saw it. In fact, one professor was in complete awe over it. Gabe felt on top of the world that day and for many days afterward.

Sara came running out of the house. "I can go, Gabe, but I have to be home by dinner time." She smiled.

"Great, let's go," Gabe said, and the two headed for his car.

###

Around six o'clock, Gabe dropped Sara off and then returned home to find his mother in the back yard. Gabe's eyes grew larger. "Mother, what are you doing out here? It's so windy!" Gabe quickly pulled down his sleeves. His hair was blowing so hard that he could barely see. He tried in vain to keep it out of his face.

"I'm doing something I should have done years ago. When you were a little boy," she said, and turned to face Gabe, "I used to take you out here when I worked on my garden. You know, I had the best flowers this side of Route 58. That's since changed with all the florists opening up after that new cemetery was built—but anyway, I'm out here as part of my therapy, and I haven't felt better in years. You probably don't remember this, but your father and I planted that tree in the front of the house. Seeing it reminded me of what I once was. Now why don't you come over here and help your mother," Martha said as she waved a soil-covered glove at Gabe.

"Listen, Mother, I'd love to stay out here with you and work on the garden, but I'm starving and want to get started on dinner."

"Dinner, you don't have to worry about that—I've already started it. A stew is cooking as we speak. I dug up an old recipe from generations ago," she said, smiling.

Gabe shook his head. He wasn't used to his mother smiling, no less acting so nice and doing all she had been. Instead of feeling happy, he was starting to feel as useless as a broken-down car. "Listen, Mom. Could I skip the garden thing? I have lots of homework to do." Gabe struggled to regain his balance as the wind continued to blow.

Martha looked up at him and said with a smile, "Sure, Gabe, go on inside and start your homework. I'll be in in a few minutes, but please keep an eye on that stew, would you."

"Sure, Mother." Gabe turned and walked toward the house, fighting the wind all the way in.

Once inside, Gabe went straight to the bathroom. A few minutes later, he was in the kitchen, looking over the stove. He stirred the thick stew with a wooden spoon. He couldn't remember when he had smelled anything so good coming from his mother's kitchen. Gabe did most of the cooking, and t*his* left a lot to be desired—he'd be the first to admit it. Gabe drank some juice out of the container. The sound of footsteps startled him; he turned around and saw his mother staring at him.

"Now you put that back and use a glass next time. Do you hear me, Gabe?" She pointed at him.

He looked at his mother and saw she was holding her dirty gloves and small digging tools. She had smears of dirt mixed with sweat on her forehead, and she looked spent.

"I need a hot bath, but I'm afraid if I take one now I'll fall asleep. I'll just wash up instead. Please continue to keep an eye on the stew, will you," she said and walked through the kitchen, tracking dirt all over the floor.

Gabe stirred the stew and brought the spoon up to his mouth for a quick taste, while looking over his shoulder for any signs of his mother. He couldn't believe it—here he had been just about living on TV dinners and canned food for the past couple of years and his mother could cook as good as this. He dropped the spoon into the stew and walked to his room.

Gabe had to have a still-life oil painting finished in two days and a perspective drawing as well. He also had a test in economics, one in English, and a paper due on Friday for art history. With it being Monday, Gabe would be busy for the rest of the week. He set up his easel, paint, and palate, and was ready to start. Gabe drew directly on the canvas, especially when doing a portrait, which he preferred to do live. Gabe worked in the old masters' style— building it up, layer upon layer. It was a painstaking way of working, but he preferred it to all other styles of painting. His latest painting was of a man dressed in black leather, holding a shiny crystal ball in his hand. Inside the ball, his reflection could be seen, along with images of other people. For the man in black's reflection, Gabe used his own face by drawing it from a mirror, but he gave the man a beard and mustache, and big red eyes that glowed like taillights on a plane.

Twenty minutes later, Gabe's mother rapped on his door. "It's time for dinner, Gabe. Now put down those paints, wash up, and get out here before your food gets cold."

He paused for a moment and had to think twice that this was not all a dream. He still found it hard to swallow how much his mother had changed and was just waiting for the floor to drop out. "I'll be right there. Just give me another minute," he said as he dabbed a few last strokes onto the canvas. Another minute turned into ten.

"Gabe, your dinner is getting cold. Now get in here before I put everything away," his mother yelled from outside his door.

He finally put down his brush, quickly washed up, and headed for the dining room. His stomach could be growling like a lion, but when he painted, nothing else seemed to matter—not even going to the bathroom. His mother had already finished eating and was washing the dishes.

"See, your dinner is cold," she said, pointing a finger at him. "Now go and warm it up in the microwave," she insisted, and waved her hand at him as if shooing away a fly.

He took a deep breath and stared at his mother. *Whenever you do this, I feel about six years old. Talk about getting on someone's nerves. I'd sooner go back to the way it was before you started to change. At least I felt in control, even though you used to nag me as much then as you do now,* he thought.

Gabe realized that that's what was eating at him—he no longer had any control over his mother. He popped in his plate and waited for the microwave to beep. As he waited, he looked over at his mother. *Could she have changed that much?* he thought, scratching his head. The phone rang.

"Hello," Martha said and wrestled with the tangled line.

She paused and looked at Gabe. "Who may I ask is calling?"

"Would you hold on while I check," she said, and cupped the phone against her chest. "Gabe, it's Sara. Do you want to take the call?" she whispered.

Gabe gasped. "Of course I do." He hurried over to his mother and grabbed the phone from her hand, giving her a look.

"Sara?" he asked. He looked on in disbelief as his mother smiled and left the kitchen without a sound—if he had tried that a month ago, she would have told him what he could do, and it would not have been nice.

"I hope you don't mind that I called. I just wanted to talk." Sara's voice faded in and out.

"Of course I don't mind. I was going to call you after dinner."

"I was wondering if you'd like to go to a school dance with me," she said hesitantly.

"A school dance," Gabe said, and thought about it. He cocked his head. "Sure, I'd love to go with you."

"Really? I wasn't sure how you'd feel about it, with us being three years apart."

"Speaking of that, have you told your family how old I am?"

"No, I haven't told them yet. I'm not sure how they'll react. They walk on the straight and narrow. Ever since my mother died, my father thinks it's necessary to watch over me like a hawk. Sometimes it's embarrassing, but Winnie always sets him straight. She's the coolest grandmother alive. Next time you come over, I'll introduce you. You'll love her."

"What a contrast we are. I was thinking about it the other day."

"Thinking about what?"

"You come from such a strong family, where I, on the other hand, come from a split one. You know, I've never met my grandparents, unless you count the time when I was born. I have no brothers or sisters, and my father . . . well, I don't know where he is. He could be dead for all I know."

"I'm sorry to hear that. So, what about your mother? Is she still getting better since meeting with that therapist you told me about?"

"She *has* broken out of her shell, but she's changed so much that sometimes I don't even recognize her—not so much in the physical sense, but more in the things she does and the way she acts. I never thought a person could change so much in such a short period of time."

"I know what you're talking about. When my mother was killed in that accident, part of me died as well. I went through a long period in which I turned inward. I might as well have been in a bubble. I've gotten over it as much as I think I can—although, on some days when I see something that reminds me of her, I may shed a tear or two. But there is also a lot of joy that goes along with thinking about her as well. As I said before, that's why my father has become so overprotective of me. But I'm also growing up, which is something he doesn't seem to understand."

"I imagine he's just trying to be a good parent. I sure wish I had *that* problem growing up," Gabe said, shaking his head.

"You know, I've never looked at it in quite that—"

"Listen, Dad's got to use the phone. So you have to get off as soon as possible," Gabe heard in the background.

"Sorry about that. It's just my sister playing around again. She's the cutest girl in the world, but boy can she be a pain in the butt when she wants to be, like when she hid in the bushes earlier today."

Gabe smiled.

"Well, I'd better get going now. I have a lot of homework to catch up on."

"Are you working at the museum tomorrow?"

"Yeah, I'll be there after school. It's supposed to rain, so a friend of the family is going to drop me off, but I'll still need a ride back."

"What time do you get off?" Gabe asked, and thought about what his day would be like tomorrow.

"I get off at six."

"My last class gets out at five, so I could pick you up at six."

"Great, I can't wait to see you again," she said, and hung up the phone.

Gabe reheated his dinner for a second time and finally ate it. He was so hungry he went back for seconds. He shook his head as he washed the dishes—he still couldn't get over how good his mother's cooking was.

"So how did the call go?"

Gabe turned to look at his mother. She had changed into a yellow nightgown and the purple bathrobe Gabe had gotten for her last Christmas.

"Fine. It was my friend from the museum. You know, the one I told you about," he said, soaping up the last of the dishes.

Martha grinned. "Oh come on, you can tell me about her." She took a cup off the shelf.

"There's nothing to tell, Mother. She's just a friend." He dropped a dish in the sink, nearly breaking it. He took a deep breath and reached for it.

"Listen, I'm doing my best to change my life, the least you can do is be honest with me," she hissed. Now *that* was the mother Gabe was used to, not the pleasant version of her that had been parading around here for the last couple of weeks.

"You have to stop at the pharmacy tomorrow after school. My new prescription is empty, and I'm afraid of what would happen if I skipped taking my pills for a day. I haven't felt this good, well, since before you were born," Martha said, the subject of Gabe's friend apparently forgotten. She put some water on for her coffee. "I'll call it in at Burke's Pharmacy first thing in the morning."

Gabe looked at his mother and just about snarled. He felt hurt by her words: *I haven't felt this good, well, since before you were born.*

Gabe clenched his fists. "Listen, Mother. Couldn't I go early in the morning? I've got plans right after school tomorrow." He dried the last dish and placed it in the cabinet.

"The pharmacy is already closed, so the earliest I could call it in would be tomorrow morning at eight o'clock. I just kept putting it off until I saw I had no pills left this afternoon. I also need some more aspirin for the pain in my head. I guess nothing can cure that. I'm really sorry, Gabe, but I need my pills. It normally takes a couple of hours to fill the prescription, so I guess if you can get there any time after twelve o'clock, it'll be ready."

Gabe slammed the cabinet door closed, rattling the glasses inside. "Mother, I told you I've got plans. I already told Sara that I'd pick her up after work, and I've got a full day of classes that will make it just about impossible to get over to the pharmacy unless I go on my lunch break," he said in his own defense—but he knew what was coming next, new mother or not.

"What's more important—picking up a friend or picking up my prescription?" she asked in a huff as she waited by the stove for the water to boil.

He dried his hands and turned to look at his mother. "Don't worry about your medicine. I'll pick it up tomorrow. You just remember to call it in in the morning, because I don't want to be waiting around all day when I do get there." Gabe threw the towel on the counter and stormed out of the kitchen.

CHAPTER SIX

Gabe's advanced-painting class had just ended. He hurriedly packed up his supplies and then headed for the door.

"Gabe, do you have a minute?" his professor asked.

"No, not really, but go ahead." Gabe stopped just before going out the door.

"Have a seat. This will only take a minute." Professor Lift marched back and forth in front of the blackboard as he did when lecturing. The man was as tall as a horse, and thin as a pencil. He sported a pair of black-rimmed glasses with coke-bottle lenses. "Let me just say that I wanted to speak to you today because I care about you." He stopped and sat down next to Gabe. He barely fit into the student chair. "Is something wrong?" His eyes did not blink as he spoke.

Gabe took a deep breath and gazed at him. "What do you mean?"

"Is there something going on that you'd like to talk to me about? Your work for the past couple of weeks has just not been up to the standards that I know you've set for yourself. I haven't seen this sort of trend in your work in the two years I've known you."

"Listen, aren't there any other students who could use your wisdom?" Gabe snapped. In his opinion, he could paint better than Professor Lift with his eyes closed, or better than any other student in the class, for that matter. Therefore, he resented any questioning of his talent.

Professor Lift pushed his black-framed glasses up with his middle finger. His puffy red eyes still did not blink. "Listen, I'm only trying to help."

Gabe looked at the clock on the wall and realized he was running late. He still had to get his mother's prescription, and then pick Sara up at the museum. "Listen, I'd love to sit and chat, but I've got things to do. Can I go?" He picked up his supplies and intended to leave no matter what the professor had to say.

Professor Lift waved his arm and shook his head as Gabe headed out of the classroom.

By the time Gabe had his books and supplies loaded into the car, it was already 5:20. He now only had twenty-five minutes to get to the pharmacy if he were to pick Sara up from work by 6:00. Halfway there, Gabe decided he would pick Sara up first and *then* get his mother's prescription.

###

At exactly 6:00, Sara came out the back door of the museum and ran to Gabe's car in the pouring rain. She covered her head with her backpack but was still soaking wet by the time she got inside.

"Well, I hope my books stayed dry," she said, putting her green backpack on the floor. "I'm glad you could make it. I would have had to wait at least an hour before my father could pick me up. He's always working late." Sara combed her wet hair back with her fingers.

"Well, I said I'd pick you up, so here I am. But before we head over to your house, I've got to stop by the pharmacy to pick up my mother's prescription," Gabe said, heading out of the parking lot.

"Which one are we going to?"

The car went over the last of the speed bumps, which had caused plenty of cups of coffee to spill in the short time the museum had been open.

"Burke's Pharmacy on 58. He's about the best there is. Not only that, but my mother doesn't trust anyone else."

"Burke's *is* one of the best around, but he closes at six o'clock sharp. No ifs, ands, or buts," Sara replied, shaking her head.

"At six?" Gabe stopped for a red light and looked at his watch. "But it's already three minutes after." Rain pounded the windshield and a gusting wind rocked the car.

"If you have the prescription with you, we can bring it to that new shopping center on Westwood Drive. There's a new drug store there that's trying to beat the competition. They stay open till seven."

Gabe shook his head and pounded the steering wheel. "We can't do that." When the light switched to green, he stepped on the gas pedal, making the tires spin. "My mother called it in over the phone this morning. I don't even know exactly what I'm picking up. I think it's called Zoltol, or something like that."

Gabe raced through the rain-soaked streets toward Sara's house.

Sara turned and looked at Gabe. "You can stop by your house first, just to let your mother know you couldn't get her prescription. What if she's waiting? When my mother died, the doctor prescribed antidepressants. Without them, I would have been a mess."

I want her to wait, especially after the way she's changed, not to mention the things she's kept from me about my father, he thought.

"I would have gone earlier to get her prescription, but I was so busy with school." Gabe came to a skidding stop at another red light. The rain was letting up, so the wiper blades squeaked every other swipe.

"Let's at least stop at a pay phone and give her a call. It'll only take a minute."

Gabe took a deep breath and shook his head. "Why do you care so much? You don't even know my mother." *And if you did, you wouldn't be so nice to her,* he thought.

Sara stared straight ahead as the light changed to green. Gabe had just shown a side of himself she hadn't seen before. She knew Gabe's relationship with his mother wasn't the best from what he had told her—she could see that every time he spoke about her, but today was different.

"Just give her a call—it'll make me feel better." She pushed her wet hair out of her face.

"Okay. Okay."

Gabe sat up straight and pulled over at the first pay phone he spotted, which was right next to the Dollar Vacuum Cleaner across from Phil's Gas-Mart. He pulled up to the phone so he could make the call from his car. He reached into his ashtray and fetched two quarters.

"Would you like something to drink?" Sara asked him.

"Yeah, I'll have an orange juice."

"One orange juice coming up." She got out of the car and headed for the Gas-Mart.

Gabe dialed the phone. He knew his mother would be screaming mad, so with that in mind, a large grin appeared on his face. The phone rang and rang, but she didn't answer. He tried again, but still no answer.

A few minutes later, Sara opened the door and got in. "Here's your juice," she said, handing the small bottle to him. She opened a can of grape soda for herself. "Did you get through?" Sara sipped her soda and burped quietly into her hand. "Excuse me."

Gabe opened his juice. "I've called twice, and the phone just keeps ringing." He shrugged.

"Why don't you try again. Maybe she was asleep or taking a shower."

"I guess." He took a sip of juice and squinted. "Now, that's cold."

Gabe dialed again and let it ring ten times, and then on the eleventh, when he was just about to hang up, he heard someone pick up the receiver. "Hello," Gabe said. No answer. "Hello," he repeated, and this time he could hear faint breathing.

Sara took a deep breath. "Is she all right?"

Gabe shrugged and shook his head. "I'm not sure. Someone picked up, but all I hear is breathing." He shuddered—hundreds of tiny fingers seemed to crawl across his back. Every scenario came to mind—especially one in which his mother was lying on the floor badly hurt. "We've got to get to my house." Gabe hung up the phone, rolled up the window, and started the car.

His back tires screeched as he floored the gas pedal. Some of Sara's soda spilled in her lap, and Gabe's juice fell to the floor. He continued to speed, even though the rain started coming down strong again. He raced through town as if he were late for his own wedding. Sara looked on as Gabe nearly crashed the car. She snapped her seat belt strap twice. The back of the car fish-tailed and the tires screamed when he turned one corner, but he appeared not to notice as he continued to race along the slick streets. Sara had a white-knuckled grip on the seat.

"Gabe, take it easy. We want to get there in one piece," she said to no avail. Gabe did not say a word as he maneuvered the car as if he, the street, and it, were one. Sara held on, mouth shut, and eyes glued to the street.

Gabe's mind ran wild. He feared the worst—that his mother was dead. With that in mind, he stepped on the pedal even harder. His old Chevy pumped as it once did twenty years ago, in its heyday. Gabe pushed his car to the limit, which almost blew the engine. He flew through yet another stop sign and went through a red traffic light. Sara had her right hand frozen to the door handle. The rain now fell even harder, making it difficult to see, but Gabe knew the roads like his own neighborhood. He pulled up to a small ranch that looked more deserted than lived in, parked half on the grass, and sprang from the car. He slipped in the mud, got back up, and ran into the house. Sara followed quickly but managed to keep her footing.

"Mother?" Gabe called out into the dark house. He quickly flipped on the lights in the living room. "Mother?" He could see she wasn't watching TV. "Mother?" he said for a third time as he looked in the bathroom. *The phone*, he thought, and raced to the kitchen.

He saw her legs sticking out in the hallway leading to the kitchen. For a moment, he didn't know what to do, but then he rushed to her side. She was lying on her stomach, groaning, and slowly moving her fingers. A few seconds later, Sara stood behind Gabe with her mouth open. She folded her arms and stared.

"Mother, what happened?" He let out a deep breath and said, "Thank God you're conscious."

"Leave me alone," she mumbled. Gabe bent down to pick her up but her body went limp. Now she was dead weight in his arms. He carefully placed her on the floor.

Sara looked down at the both of them and said, "Why don't I call the ambulance. Where's the phone?" She looked up.

She's gonna hate me for doing this, he thought.

"It's on the wall by the back door," Gabe said and pointed.

Sara turned to see a cream-colored rotary phone on the wall. She hurried to it, picked up the dangling receiver, clicked the holder, and dialed 911. She asked for an ambulance, told them what had happened, and then gave Gabe's address. She then rushed back to Gabe. "They're on their way." Sara reached for his hand and firmly held it.

Fearing she might not be able to breathe right, Gabe let go of Sara's hand and turned his mother over. He knew he could hurt her even more, but he couldn't just sit there and do nothing.

"She's so warm."

"I'll get something cold for her head."

When Sara had called 911, she had seen the sink and a small white dishcloth draped over it. She let the cold water run and passed the cloth under it, then wrung it out. She walked over to Gabe and handed it to him. "Here, put this on her forehead."

"Thanks," he said and did just that. He looked at his mother lying on the floor and wondered what could have happened.

"Where are they?"

"Gabe, it's only been a few minutes. Don't worry, she'll be all right," Sara assured him as she again held his hand, which eased him.

Three minutes later, sirens could be heard, and then a loud knock on the door.

"They're here, Gabe. You stay put, and I'll let them in." Sara sprang up to answer the door, and along the way, she flipped on as many lights as she could.

"She's over in the kitchen, to your left, just around the corner." Sara held the door open for the two EMTs to get their equipment in.

Reality set in when Gabe saw the two technicians roll in a stretcher. His nerves were at an all-time high, and no handholding could do a thing about it now. Gabe knelt on the floor and wouldn't budge.

"You're going to have to please move out of the way," a woman EMT with a swollen red nose and waxy complexion said. She checked Martha's pulse while her partner opened his orange box of supplies.

Sara walked away from the small group that was now setting up camp on Gabe's kitchen floor. "Gabe, why don't you come with me. Your mother is in good hands now."

Sara waved Gabe over, and he walked toward her, though he stayed close enough to see what they were doing. He suddenly covered his face and ran to the bathroom. When he came back, his eyes were bloodshot. "Sorry about that." He looked away.

"Don't worry about it. I know how it feels when you care for someone."

Gabe looked at her. "You don't know the half of it. I've wished my mother dead more times than I care to admit, but seeing her like this scared the hell out of me. Now I wish I had never thought such a thing." He almost burst into tears again but managed to keep them at bay. The EMTs strapped his mother to a long board and were just about ready to roll her out.

Martha's eyelids fluttered, and she raised her head. "Who are you?"

Gabe stood at her side. "Mother, they're just taking you to the hospital. It looks like you had a fall."

"Taking me where? You know how much I hate hos—" Her voice trailed off, and she tried to sit up, but the EMT with the red nose placed her hand on Martha's chest.

"Sorry, you have to come with us now," she insisted.

"I want to go with her," Gabe said and held out his hand.

The EMT looked at Gabe and said, "Sure, you can ride in the back with her."

"Sara, can you drive?"

"If you mean legally, no, I can't. But I can handle a car."

Gabe didn't think a second more about it as he reached into his pocket. "Here are the keys to my car. You can follow us if you'd like, or you can wait here for me. I guess I could take a cab back home."

"No, I'll follow."

Gabe told her to stay close in case she got pulled over—the police would surely have to understand.

Inside the ambulance, Gabe found out that his mother had probably just fainted and hit her head. But that still didn't ease the guilt he felt inside—but, then again, what could?

###

Two and a half hours later, when he found out that his mother was in stable condition, Gabe left the hospital. But he was still on edge.

The drive with Sara was deafening in its silence. Even the rain had stopped and the wind had died down. Gabe finally spoke. "You know, it's my fault she passed out in the first place. If I had picked up her prescription earlier in the day, this would never have happened." He let out a deep sigh.

"You don't know that," Sara said as she rolled down the window. "People faint and hit their heads all the time."

"You don't understand. The doctor asked me a few questions, and when I told him about my mother's prescription and why she was taking it, he said her not having it could have caused her to faint and hit her head."

"See, you said it yourself. 'Could have caused' is a big difference from 'caused.' I think you should give yourself a break and get a good night's sleep. I'm gonna try and do the same when I get home."

"Thanks, Sara. I don't know what I would've done if you weren't here today." Gabe slid his hand over to hers. He looked down at her hand and held it tightly. Gabe knew he was falling hard for her. He just hoped it would work out.

Gabe continued down Route 58 to Sara's house. This particular stretch of road had no streetlights—the only light at all came from the moon and a few passing cars. Gabe suddenly had an urge to pull over and park the car.

"What's wrong?" Sara asked, and pulled her hand away.

"Nothing," he said and got out of the car. "Just look at them—all those tiny points of light so many years old." Gabe walked in circles as he pointed up at the sky.

"What are you doing?" Sara asked as she slammed the car door behind her.

He laughed and walked away. "Sara, come on. I've got something to show you."

Sara stood motionless with her hands at her sides. "Come back here. Don't leave me alone, Gabe. I hate to be alone in the dark when I'm in a strange place." Her voice quivered. But he didn't answer. "Listen, Gabe. If you don't come back, I'm going to get in the car and drive away." But she didn't have the keys; they were in Gabe's pants pocket.

Gabe was now too far from Sara to hear her. He stood inside the windmill where he had seen the tall man a few days ago. The moon provided some light, but he still could not see that well. He started banging on the walls of the old windmill. "Come out, birds. Come out and play with Gabe." He pounded one fist into the other. "I said come out and playyyyyyy," he added with a sneer.

None were forthcoming.

"Go to hell, you damn birds," Gabe hissed. He sat down on the dirt floor and thought about how much he hated the way his life was. Soon, tears fell from his tired eyes, but he quickly wiped them away. He looked up to find that one bird had answered his call and started crowing the minute it entered the windmill. Soon two, then four, and then well over twenty birds filled the place. Gabe couldn't believe how many birds were now inside the windmill. The wind picked up and blew hard, whistling through the broken boards and wood that held the old vane together. Gabe thought of poor Charley Eaton—then he began to scream. A bird then pecked at his face and he swung his hand frantically, batting it away. He started yelling at the birds again, blaming them for all the bad things that had happened in his life.

"Mother, Mother, it's not my fault."

Then he realized that Sara had not joined him in the windmill, and he ran from the place as fast as he could. In the distance, his car's shiny chrome bumpers glittered like a lighthouse. He could make out the outline of a person standing in front of the Chevy. He paused and stared.

"Gabe, is that you? Are you all right?" Sara took a few steps forward, the wind steadily building.

A few seconds later, the sound of crunching dirt and rocks filled the air—someone or something was coming. Sara stood straight and glared at the space in front of her. She stepped back a few feet and again stood motionless. The crunching sounds grew louder and faster.

"It has to be," she said aloud. "Yes, it is." Her fear turned to relief. "Gabe, what's going on? You know, you just about scared the hell out of me," she said as she saw his frightened face.

Blood trickled down his cheek, and he looked a ghostly white. His eyes opened wide when he saw her. "Sara, I'm sorry about all of this." He sat down in the mud by her feet. "Did you see them?" he asked looking up, almost laughing. "Did you see all of them in the sky, black as ink? They looked like one big dark shadow when they moved. I hate those damn birds—those beady black eyes dancing the way they do." Gabe fought to catch his breath.

"Gabe, what are you talking about?" Sara asked a second too soon. The resonance of birds flying overhead filled the air—it sounded like a million people turning pages in a book. The sound seemed to last forever as the birds continued to move overhead, but it slowly dissipated.

Sara stared at them. "My God, how many birds *were* there?" She bent down and hugged Gabe tightly. "I've never seen that many in my life."

The birds passed over the lemon-yellow crescent moon. Sara closed her eyes and shuddered.

"You know, you just about scared the life out of me. Let's get out of here," she said and let go of him.

Gabe was trying to figure out what had just happened himself. His skin was covered in a light glaze of sweat, and his heart still thumped in his temples. Sara had already walked toward the car. Gabe quickly followed. Inside, the car was filled with tension. They got back onto 58 and headed toward Sara's house.

"I'm sorry," came out of Gabe's mouth with the force of a dying wind. "I don't know what came over me." He looked away.

Sara shook her head. "It's okay. I guess you were just stressed out over what happened to your mother—though I think you'd better take it easy until all of this blows over."

"That sounds like a good idea, Sara, but I don't know. My life has been this way for such a long time, ever since I can remember. My mother isn't an ordinary person. I wish I knew what mold she was cut from so that I could break it. She's caused me so much pain, and I'm not sure she even knows how much." Gabe looked out the window.

The street was dark. Not even a single car had passed them, but a deer shot out from the side of the road to the other. Gabe stopped the car with a skid. He looked both ways and watched the deer disappear into the darkness. "You know, last year I hit a doe. When I saw the trail of blood, I thought I killed it. I've been told they can take a buck shot and run for hundreds of yards before they drop and die. It sure did smash up my car pretty good. If you look, you can see the dent it made on the hood. I banged out the rest," he said, trying to loosen the tension. "After all that's happened today, I hope you still want to see me again—though I wouldn't be surprised if you don't." Gabe gripped the steering wheel.

Sara sat there and didn't move or say a word.

Gabe felt this was the end of the line for Sara and him. He had to admit that it did happen in a way he could have never imagined.

Gabe passed the shooting range, which meant Sara's house was only a few minutes more away. His nerves twitched. He hoped this wouldn't be the last time he'd see her. Sara looked at the tall spruce tree that stood to the left of her house, and let out a deep breath. Gabe slowly pulled into her driveway, parked behind her father's old Ford pickup, and left the engine running. A bright spotlight from the front of the house automatically went on and lit up most of the blacktop driveway.

"Well, I guess this is it," he said, looking at her.

Sara leaned over toward Gabe and kissed him full on the mouth. She pulled away and said, "I'll call you, but please give me some time. I'm gonna need it." She got out of the car and slowly walked up the driveway.

CHAPTER SEVEN

Two days had passed since Gabe's mother had fainted and hit her head at the house, and Gabe had only gone to see her once at the hospital. Martha wasn't at the blaming stage—not yet, anyway. Other than Gabe, his mother didn't have any visitors. That in itself didn't bother her, but Mr. McMillan, the man in the bed next to her who had had a heart attack, had more visitors than the president of the United States. *That* she just couldn't take.

Around eleven thirty, Emily stopped by. At this point, she'd see anyone. "Mrs. Chaplin, how are you doing today?" Emily pulled up a chair and sat next to Martha's bed.

"I guess I'm okay," Martha said, struggling to sit up. "To tell you the truth, the food stinks, the service is always late, and I need my pills—you know, the ones you prescribed for me. They did wonders for my condition, and I can't wait to take them again." Martha smiled.

Emily paused. "That's why I'm here. The pills may have caused you to faint in the first place. I just spoke with your doctor, and he's having some tests done. But he too confirmed that's probably what happened. It's just that I've never heard of any side effects like fainting before." Emily shook her head.

"What am I going to do now? It's like having something you

waited all your life for and then having it snatched away. There has to be another medication that I could take that would do the same thing. Isn't there?" Martha's face became red, and her eyes swelled with tears. "I haven't felt this good in years. Please don't take that away from me," Martha pleaded.

Tears fell from her eyes. She quickly dried them with a tissue, but they wouldn't stop. After soaking a handful of them, they finally did, but not after she had sniffled and wiped her nose. "I'm sorry about this, but it's not every day that your life is given back to you and then taken away just as quickly." Martha blew again.

"I know how you must feel, but believe me, I'll do my best to find another medication for you. Have you spoken to Gabe about this?"

Martha looked away. "Gabe? No I haven't," she said as if it now hurt to speak. "The nurse said he stopped by yesterday, but I was in a deep sleep on account of a pain killer they gave me. I think she said he'll be back some time today. I still blame him for the bump on the back of my head. If he had gotten my medication in the first place, none of this would have happened." She folded her arms and took a deep breath.

"Mrs. Chaplin," Emily said and leaned closer to the bed, "your son had nothing to do with this—it would have happened regardless of what he did. Just try to keep that in mind. Remember the headaches you told me about?" Martha nodded. "Well, they were the start of your problems with the medication I had prescribed for you."

"That's not the point," Martha said and reached for a cup of water that was on the table to her right. "I knew he wasn't going to go like I had asked. We had an argument over it the night before. And now I see he's got a girlfriend." She quickly took a sip of water. The veins in her neck throbbed.

"When are you going home?" Emily asked, and pulled a small black leather book and a gold pen out of her pocket.

"They say I can probably go home after all the tests are in, which should be no longer than a few more days at most. They just want to make sure the fall didn't hurt anything in here," she said and tapped her skull. "I told them there wasn't much in there to begin with anyway."

Emily chuckled. "Then you should be home by the beginning of next week."

"If everything goes as planned, yes."

Emily looked over her schedule. "I can meet with you Tuesday or Wednesday, between twelve and one o'clock. Would that be all right with you?"

"If I'm home by then, sure. But can you come out to my place? I don't know if I'll be able to get a ride over to your office," Martha said as Mr. McMillan started to cough as if he was choking.

"Sure, I can come out and see you." Emily put away her pen and pad. "Now, you take it easy," she said and got up. "And by the way, if you find out when you're getting out, do call and let me know in case we have to reschedule our appointment. And do get some rest," Emily added, and then left the room.

Martha lay there, staring at the ceiling. "Why me? What did I ever do?" She slammed the bed, grabbed the sheets, and started to cry.

###

Gabe was at home, putting the finishing touches on a painting he was doing for class. In it, a row of windmills stretched far back into the horizon, and in the foreground, a wheat field was in full bloom. Gabe had painted it so well you could hear the tall brown strands swaying back and forth. The painting was dark, except for the light the three-quarter moon provided. Looking closely at the painting, you could see black birds everywhere—the foreground, the background, and in the sky as well. In front of all of this stood a large windmill that took up over half of the three-by-four-foot canvas. The windmill was in the shape of a black bird with glowing red eyes, and a streak of gray running down its back. Its blades looked like feathers. Gabe called it *Black Birds at Night*. Its overall hue was a dark bluish tone. He must have used half a tube of paynes gray to paint the sky a dark, dull silver.

Gabe glanced at the clock on the wall and saw that it was
4:30. Visiting hours started at 6:30, so he had time to wash up,
eat, and head over to see his mother. Every time Gabe passed the
phone, he wanted to call Sara, but she did say she needed some
time, and Gabe was going to give it to her.

Standing in the kitchen, getting something to eat, the phone
rang. Gabe nearly jumped out of his shoes and rushed to answer
it. He was all set to hear Sara's serene voice.

"Gabe, I hope you're stopping by tonight. I can't stand being
cooped up in this place another minute."

Gabe could hear the television in the background. "I see you've
got the tube on. You can't go a minute without it, can you, Mother?"
He shook his head.

"It looks like they're going to keep me here until Monday
morning, maybe Tuesday. They're telling me that all the test results
have to be in before they can let me go, but I really think they're
just after more money from my insurance company. You wouldn't
believe how many tests I've had. I'm surprised I have any blood
left pumping in my veins. Can you believe that? And what if I had
to pay for this myself?" She sighed.

"Well at least you have insurance, Mother. Is there anything
you'd like for me to bring?" Gabe asked, without even thinking.

"I'd like for you to bring my pink sweater. It's deathly cold in
here. Second, I'd appreciate it if you'd bring me a TV guide—I'd
like to know what's on TV tonight. You can also bring me a change
of clothes and underthings, though I don't care what you bring in
that department. And one last thing—I'd love a box of salt-water
taffy. You can get that here at the thrift shop. You know how
much I just love taffy."

"Is that all, Mother?"

"No. Could you also bring me my pocketbook? I've got to give
them some information before I can check out of here." Martha
could be nice, especially when she wanted something. Gabe knew
her little game but gave her the benefit of a doubt, but he wasn't
holding his breath.

"I've got to shower and have a bite to eat. So I'll be over around six thirty."

"Okay Gabe, but don't forget my stuff, or I'll send you right back home to get it. Do you understand me?" Her voice rose higher like an opera singer.

Gabe sighed and said, "Of course I do!" He hung up the phone and just stood there, thinking about nothing.

Gabe showered, gathered his mother's things, and had to settle for a Stouffer's potpie for dinner, because the microwave was on the fritz again. The oven was also a problem, but today it worked, black soot stove and all. Gabe stalled as much as he could, hoping Sara would call, but it was getting late. With no hope that she would, Gabe hit the road to go and visit his mother.

For the past two days, it had rained without a sign that it would ever stop, but finally it did. The crops of Southwick would thank the heavens, as would the farmers for the rain.

Gabe made it to the hospital with ten minutes to spare. He knew he'd better not be late this time. He parked his car under a tall bumpy oak tree with its twisted branches reaching for the golden globe in a cloudless sky. Everyone in town was outside doing chores, tending to their lawns, and enjoying the crisp spring day.

Once inside the hospital, he found out where his mother was staying and took the elevator up to room 326. He also made sure to get the taffy at the thrift shop. On the way up in the elevator, he rode with an old couple who bickered back and forth as if they were mortal enemies. Gabe shook his head, got out of the elevator, and passed the nurses' station on route to his mother's room. He flashed a smile in their direction, but they were too busy to notice. When he approached his mother's room, his footsteps became slower and shorter, as if it hurt to bend his knees. He stopped at the doorway and gave a few knocks at a door that was slightly open.

"Is that you, Gabe?"

Gabe walked in. "Hi, Mother," he said, and put the bag with her things down at the foot of her bed.

She had been sleeping for the past two hours—the creases in her face and the sand in her eyes said as much. But in no time, she was wide awake.

"Give it here," she said and pointed to the bag. Gabe picked it up and quickly handed it to her. She searched through the bag as if it were filled with treasures. She looked up. "You remembered everything, even the taffy. I'm proud of you, Son. You know who came to see me yesterday?" She smiled and put the bag down on her lap. She didn't even wait for Gabe to answer. "Emily . . . though she didn't have any good news for me. She said I can't take the medication she prescribed for me any more, so you can forget about what happened to me ever being your fault. Both she and the doctor said it would have happened regardless if I had my medication or not. They're looking for something else I can take, something that won't upset my balance like it did. The doctor was amazed it didn't happen any sooner."

Gabe smiled. This was just what he wanted to hear—he would now have his old mother back. At least that's what he hoped for. As his mother had said, however, there was always the chance that they might find another drug to replace the one she had been taking.

Gabe walked over to the window and opened the blinds. Light from the sun setting streamed in, filling her side of the room with a warm orange and reddish glow. "It's so beautiful outside, Mother," he said as he thought about Sara and how shiny her hair looked when the sun hit it just right. He could just about smell her sweet scent.

"Listen, Gabe. On Monday, I'm probably going to need a ride home. I hope you can take me," she said as she thumbed through the TV guide he had brought. "You know how much I hate cabs—bastards don't know how to drive worth a damn!"

Gabe turned away from the window, looked at his mother, and walked over to her. "I can't wait around all day. I've got classes to attend," he said in a rather loud voice, and stood over her.

Her lip curled and her brow furrowed. Martha dropped the TV Guide and gave Gabe a look he knew all too well. "I see you still don't care much about your mother." Martha frowned and looked away. "I should have known as much. It's all your fault I'm here anyway. I never asked to be taken to the hospital just for a bump on my head." She folded her arms.

"Are you nuts? I was just making sure you weren't hurt. When I saw you lying on the floor, what was I supposed to think?" Gabe gasped. Martha's eyebrows rose. "Why don't you take a taxi home, Mother," Gabe insisted, like so many times before.

"I've already told you I don't like cabs. But I do know what you're up to. You're thinking if I take a cab this time I might be the next, and so on and so on. I know the way you think, Gabe. You just don't care about me." She shook her head.

"How can you say that? If we hadn't found you when we did, who knows what could have happened." Gabe scowled at her.

She threw her arms to the air and said, "You've got to be kidding. Are you trying to say that you saved my life? All I had was a bump on the back of my head the size of a golf ball, and you saved my life." She paused and added in the sharpest tone, "We? Who was with you that day?" she said as she squinted at him.

Gabe moved away from the bed and looked out the window again. On the street below, an ambulance was pulling in. "I was with Sara—you know, the girl I told you I was picking up after school." He looked over his shoulder and waited for his mother's wrath.

"So that's why you were late. I should have known as much. Girls are trouble, Gabe. How many times do I have to tell you? You're only going to get hurt," she said, shaking her head and mumbling words to herself.

Still looking out the window, Gabe said, "You don't have to worry about her—I don't think we're going to see each other any longer."

"Well that's good news for you. You don't need any more hurting," she said with a smile. Gabe knew that he was all she had and she didn't want him leaving her anytime soon.

Gabe moved away from the window, thinking that nobody could cause him as much pain as his mother had and would continue to do. "Mother," he said as he stood at her bedside for the second time. "I'm not a little boy any more. The day will come when I've got to leave. Surely, you must know that. I can't stay home forever.

I've got to fly on my own sooner or later." Gabe took a deep breath and looked down at the floor.

"Why do you speak like this? Especially when your mother is lying on her back in a hospital bed. I've got enough things to worry about without you talking about leaving me. Now, you come over here and give your mother a kiss on the cheek."

"Mother, would you please." Gabe walked over to her and bent so she could kiss him on the cheek. She smiled.

"They'll be bringing in my dinner in about ten minutes. You don't know how much I hate hospital food. You know, they said I need exercise to get my blood flowing, but I'm not well enough to walk just yet." Whenever Gabe spoke about leaving, she would always defuse the moment just as she did this time. However, her reins on him were getting thin as spider webs.

###

Five minutes later, Gabe left the hospital wondering about Sara—on the way home he stopped by the museum to see if she was in, but she wasn't. He parked out back and looked for her bike, but he couldn't find it. He stayed there, sitting in his car with the windows open, enjoying the sun as it beamed down on his face. He deeply inhaled the fresh air that only Southwick could provide. He flipped on the radio, moving from station to station. When he came upon Pastor William F. Honeycomb's talk radio religion show, he let the dial sit. The pastor was fond of saying that the world would soon come to an end if folks didn't all repent their sins and live the way God wanted them to. He had a booming voice that sounded like a megaphone. Gabe wasn't much of a religious person—he was Catholic by birth, but other than going to Sunday school a long time ago, he hadn't stepped near a church since.

"Ye sins must be repented," Pastor Honeycomb bellowed. The cone of Gabe's speakers vibrated with every word the pastor spoke. "Our Lord died for our sins once and it won't happen again. We must now pick up the burden he carried for us so long ago."

"Yes sir, yes sir," a chorus of voices echoed in his studio every time he stopped speaking.

"God is forgiving, that is, if you let him into your heart. You must want God every day. Not just when you're down and out."

"Tell them, Pastor Honeycomb," the chorus went. "Tell them."

"Come to the church on Westwood Drive and let God free you of your contempt." He spoke as if he were talking directly to each person who was listening.

A loud applause broke out, as did the twang of a keyboard, and the unison of seemingly hundreds of voices harmonizing as one. Gabe laughed and turned it off. Out in the country, there were plenty of people like Pastor Honeycomb. And with the new millennium already begun, they'd be crawling out from the woodwork to warn everyone of the destruction that would accompany it.

Gabe started the car and was going to head home, but a tall figure dressed in a long dark gray trench coat that ruffled in the breeze approached the car. Gabe swallowed hard and shivered. The tall man stood outside his car and knocked on the window. A smooth gold ring glittered from the sun. Gabe reluctantly reached for the handle and rolled down the window.

"I see you're waiting for Sara. I guess you didn't listen to what I had to say," the tall man said and looked down at Gabe.

"Why are you stalking her?" Gabe asked and shivered.

The tall man stretched his arms out and rested them on the rooftop of Gabe's car. "It's best that you don't know why."

Gabe brought his hand up and grabbed the steering wheel. "Really? I do know whatever she is, it's special, and I also know you can't do a thing about it, because if you could, you would have already done so." Gabe tilted his head. "So what do you want from me?"

The tall man laughed. "Now, isn't that the million-dollar question. I told you to stay away from her, and you did not listen. She will fill your mind with shameless stories. That's how she starts out." His black bushy eyebrows rose. "Soon you will not be able to pull away. All that you know and all that you do will be for her, and her only."

"She's none of that. Surely, you must have the wrong person."
Gabe shook his head.

The tall man bent down and looked at Gabe through the open
window. His black hair danced from a building wind. "She is the
right person. *That* you can count on." He shook a long bony finger
at Gabe. "Time is of the essence, so I would not waste much more
on her. I'll be close by, so watch yourself."

With that, the tall man turned and walked back to the museum.

Gabe leaned his head out of the window and screamed, "Stop
following me! Do you hear me? Stop it!" The tall man raised both
his arms, smiled, and waved.

Gabe took a few deep breaths and quickly rolled up the
windows. He looked at himself in the rearview mirror. "Now, when
did you start to become so brave?" Gabe gazed back at himself and
laughed.

CHAPTER EIGHT

The next morning, Sara stood in her driveway, looking at the clear blue sky. She looked to be deep in thought.

"So what happened to your friend? I thought we were supposed to start working on the car this weekend."

Sara looked down at her father who was changing the oil and said, "You mean Gabe? I don't think I'll be seeing him anymore." The wind blew her hair in her face, and she pushed it out of the way.

"That's a shame. I thought he was a nice boy," he said, and rolled back under the car. "Pumpkin, could you hand me the wrench?" he asked and stuck out an oil-stained hand.

Sara bent down and picked up the shiny wrench. "Here you go, Dad."

Sara's father tightened the drain plug and slid out from under the car. Sara had her back to him, looking off into nowhere.

"I think you should give this boy another chance," Johnny said and wiped his hands clean with a pink rag he took from his back pocket. "Sometimes you have to give people a second chance."

Sara looked at her father. "You know, you're right. I'm going to give him a call right now." She thanked her father and ran to the house.

Inside, she quickly dialed Gabe's number. It rang five times, and when she was about to give up, someone picked up. "Gabe," she said.

"Sara."

"Gabe, you don't know how glad I am to hear your voice. I'm sorry I took so long to call."

"There's no need to be sorry. What I pulled the other night was totally out of line, and I'm sorry if I caused you any trouble."

"I accept your apology. You know, my father was asking about you. He still thinks you're going to help him with his car. I know it needs a lot of work, but between the two of you, I know it can be done."

"I'd love to help him, but I don't know how much free time I'll have this weekend. Between mother and school, I just don't know."

"Speaking of her, how is she?"

"She's okay. She's supposed to come home early next week. They need to see all of her test results before they can officially let her go."

"Do they know what caused her to faint?"

"They do—it was most likely the new medication she was on, and now she can't take it any more. It's a double-edged sword, Sara."

"Would you care to explain that to me?"

Gabe leaned up against the kitchen wall and ran a hand through his hair. "I was used to the way my mother had been for many years, and when she changed with that medication, I just didn't know what to do. But the flip side to that is, I again have to take care of her."

"Now I know what you mean by a double-edged sword. Don't you have any relatives who live close enough to come help out now and again?"

"We have a few, but after my parents split, so did the family. They blamed my mother and never forgave her."

"What a story. How have you managed to stay there for as long as you have?"

"I've tried to leave, but I just can't leave her all alone. I just can't. She knows just how to make me feel guilty. She's an ace at that."

"I never realized how good I have it. But you've got to do something about this, Gabe, or it will destroy your life."

"I know, Sara, but it's so hard. She is my mother, and she stayed with me when I had no one."

"That may be true, but you've got to stop this chain or you'll never be able to break it. At the rate you're going, even if she died she'd still have a hold on you. Stop it now, Gabe. Stop it before it's too late. You've got a lot of living ahead of you."

"Where did such a young girl as yourself find all this wisdom?"

"I don't know. No one has ever said that to me before, so I guess I'll take that as a compliment."

Gabe laughed.

"Would you like to get together today?" Sara asked.

"Sure, I could pick you up after dinner. Would that be okay?" Gabe said, excited.

"Of course. I eat at seven just about every night, so you could pick me up around seven thirty."

"Great, I'll see you then," he said, and hung up the phone.

"Yes, yes," exclaimed Gabe as he nearly danced in the middle of the kitchen. He had thought for sure that he and Sara were over and done—especially after what happened the other night. But surprise was now the order of the day. He paused. *The tall man— I forgot to tell her about the tall man.*

###

Sara had just left the kitchen and was standing on the deck, overlooking her vast back yard. She watched the horses as they ate hay in the pen, and today there was something special about the whole scene—it had a quality of freshness to it, as if she were seeing it for the first time. Winnie followed her out, holding a cup of tea.

"So you finally called him. I was wondering how long it would take," Winnie said, and closed the sliding door behind them.

Sara turned and said, "I guess you know me better than I know myself. I don't know how I can ever thank you for all you've done. When Mom died, I thought the pain would never go away, but you saw to it that it would. Though I guess it will always be there to some degree, you've helped me to put it in its proper place." Sara walked over to her grandmother and hugged her tightly. She pulled away and smiled.

"I had a similar experience as a child—my father died in World War II. He was a great war hero, but I'd trade all of that to have had him there when I was a child. It's important for children to have good adults around them when they're growing up. That's why we have what we do today—most adults can't even take care of themselves, much less their children."

"I always wanted to ask you about him. I've seen the pictures, but I sensed you didn't want to talk about it. So I let it be," Sara said, and sat down at the redwood table her father had built last summer. Winnie sat across from her with the sun in her eyes, so that she squinted.

"You said something before about pain," Winnie said and shook her head. "I've lived a long time, and if there's one thing I've learned, it's that pain is a close friend—always lurking around, waiting for the chance to cling to you like a moth to light." Winnie blinked and coughed into her hand. "How long has my father been dead? Ten, twenty, thirty . . . he's been dead fifty-seven years and I still tear up when I speak about him. See what I mean," she said as she pulled a tissue from her apron and dabbed the corners of her eyes.

Pain was written all over Winnie's blotched and wrinkled face. "I never realized how hard this was on you," Sara said and reached out with her hands and touched Winnie's.

"Oh, look what I've gone and done. There I go, bringing you down," she said and let go of Sara's hand.

"Don't worry, Winnie. You can cry all you like." Sara smiled.

"You've sure turned out to be quite a young woman," Winnie said with a sparkle now in her eyes. "I hope I'm around to see your first book published." She pushed her lips together and opened her eyes all the way. "And don't go and give me that 'I don't write all that much' look anymore."

Sara laughed and turned when the sliding door opened. Winnie's husband, Ralph, stepped out, clutching the top of his cane.

"Miss Winnie, don't you go and lay the world on Miss Sara today. She's too young for that," he said as he made his way over to the both of them. He called every woman Miss. He too sat down, and you could hear every bone in his body crack like a knuckle. "You'd better learn something other than that writing of yours." He shook a shaky hand at Sara. "Someday you're going to have to make a living, and writing can be slim pickings. Believe me, I know. I once had a friend—Elmore James was his name. And boy could he write. He'd give *The Old Man and the Sea* a hell of a run for its money," Ralph said.

Sara and Winnie looked at each other and chuckled.

"Maybe *you* should have been a writer, old man. You sure tell enough tall tales," Winnie said, and gave Sara a wink.

"Good old Elmore, God bless his soul," Ralph said with a smile and a shake of his head. "Elmore died three years ago, and I miss him very much."

"Now you stick a sock in it, Ralphie old boy. Sara has heard enough of your wild stories. No wonder where she gets it from," Winnie said with a laugh.

"You always have to go and ruin it. So my memory isn't as good as it once was. Old age will do that to a person," he said and rocked back and forth.

Ralph was a frail man with more wrinkles on his face than on a piece of worn leather. His sea blue eyes still held the magnetism they had from the day he was born. In a room full of people, Ralph stood out, all because of his sparkling blue eyes.

"You can tell me all the stories you'd like, Grandpa," Sara said, and smiled at Winnie. Winnie returned her smile, put the tissue back in her apron, and folded her hands together on the table.

"I think this group could use some of my homemade iced tea. Now how about it?" Winnie said and got up.

"Yeah, I could go for some. How about you, Grandpa?"

"Are you going to put those lemon chunks in it?"

"Of course I am," Winnie said with that smile of hers.

After all these years, they still cared as much for each other as they did when they had first fallen in love. They had a secret language only seasoned lovers and good friends knew. All she had to do was flash a smile or burn a look and he'd know what she was thinking, and the same went for Winnie.

###

Gabe was back home working fiercely when the phone rang. "What do you mean you're coming home today?" Gabe spoke loud enough to be heard in every corner of the house. "I thought you were coming home early next week?

"I did too. But I'm glad to not have to spend the weekend here. I thought we went over this the other day. You said you'd take me home, didn't you?"

Gabe recalled telling her to take a cab that day. "What time are they letting you out?" he asked, gripping the phone almost hard enough to crack it.

"I'm still waiting for my doctor to see me. He's got the final word, but everyone else is saying it's just a formality, and that all they need is his signature to let me go."

"So you don't know when you're getting out, do you?" Gabe took a deep breath.

"No, I don't, so don't get snippy with me. I figured you'd be home working on your schoolwork anyway. Do you have a date with that girl?" she asked with scorn.

"Yes, I do."

"I thought you two were finished."

"We were, but she called me and we're back together again." Gabe smiled.

"I've told you about girls—they're only going to cause you trouble, more trouble than you can handle."

Not as much as you, he thought.

"I can't stop you from seeing her but I can stop you from bringing her into my house. Do you hear what I'm saying?" When Martha got like this, her lower lip curled like the end of a fishhook, her eyes grew larger than silver dollars, and her hands clenched like a boxer's punch.

Gabe paused for a moment, as if it had taken his mind a second to catch up to what his lips were about to say. "Listen, if it weren't for me, the house wouldn't even be here today. Who do you think took care of it for the past three years?" Gabe took a few steps away from the phone.

"Let's not get into that now. All I want is for you to stick around the house, and I'll call you later this afternoon to let you know if I'm going to need a ride home. Can you at least do that for me?"

Gabe shook his head and kicked at the floor. "All right. All right, Mother. But let the phone ring a few times—I'll be working in my room."

"Just stay around the house, Gabe, will you," she said, and hung up the phone.

Gabe slammed the phone down so hard the bell inside rang. Not knowing if he'd be able to pick Sara up later, he decided to call her to let her know he might be late. He dialed but received a busy signal. He waited a few minutes and tried again, with the same results.

I'll try later, he thought, and darted into his room to work on yet another painting. In this one, a woman with butterfly wings was sitting on a rock. The background looked like a Rembrandt— dark, with the subject matter lit up like a stage. The woman looked a bit like Sara, but this woman was naked, and Gabe hadn't seen Sara without her clothes on. He wasn't even sure he was going to show it to her. The woman's eyes were emerald green and sparkled like diamond chips. Her skin was a mix of warm colors and glazed in just the right places to simulate real flesh. Gabe had the glazing technique down. With this effect mastered, his paintings had a three-dimensional look to them.

Gabe felt there were two things he was put on this earth to

do—the first, being the painting and the second, taking care of his mother, but he was growing tired of the latter.

By the time Gabe looked at the clock, it was already past 4:30. *Surely Mother isn't going to come home this late*, he thought as he entered the kitchen, which was now filled with sunlight, so that he had to cover his eyes. He poured a glass of orange juice and warmed up a leftover hamburger from two nights ago. He sat in the kitchen with his back toward the rays of sun when he heard something at the back door. He sprang up, walked to the door, and slowly pulled the blinds aside to see what is was. Sure enough, it was his mother fumbling through her purse for the keys to the door. *How can this be? Surely, she didn't take a cab*, he thought. Seeing that his mother didn't have the key, or couldn't find it, he unlocked and opened the door.

"What are you doing home? I've been calling all afternoon. Don't you listen for the phone anymore?" She shook her head.

"Of course I do. I've been home all day painting in my room."

Martha walked over to the phone. "No wonder you didn't hear it—the phone was off the hook. How many times have I told you to do things the right way," she said and hung up the phone. "I'm gone a couple of days, and you fall to pieces," she added and took off her coat and hat, and put down her bag. Gabe had to admit, she looked to be her old self.

"Lucky I had a few bucks in my purse, or I would have been walking home," she said, glaring at Gabe. "I couldn't spend another hour in that darn place! Is there anything to eat?" She walked to the kitchen and searched through the cupboards. "I haven't had a decent meal in three days."

Gabe was relieved his mother was home; now he'd be able to go out with Sara tonight.

Martha found a box of Kraft Macaroni and Cheese and some cold cuts. She placed them both on the counter. "Have you ever tasted hospital food? It stinks! I'd die if I had to stay in there another day eating the stuff," she said and twisted her face.

"Since you're home, I guess I can go out tonight," Gabe said and took out some more orange juice from the refrigerator. Grabbing a glass off the counter, he poured himself some and sat down at the table.

"What did I tell you about girls—they're only trouble. Look what they did to your father. He shacked up with a girl, and we got divorced. Your school work is your ticket out of here." Martha filled a pot with water and dumped in the macaroni and a few dabs of salt. "Will you look at this place! How many times do I have to tell you to clean up after yourself." Dirty dishes filled the sink, so that she had a hard time getting the pot in to fill it with water.

"Speaking of my father, why did you keep the truth from me all those years?"

She looked up and shook her head. "Don't start with that now. I'm in no mood for bringing up the past. And even if I did, what can you do about it now?"

"Nothing. But you should have told me anyway. It would have put a lot of things in perspective."

"Like what? Don't you go and blame me for all your problems," she said and shook a finger at him. "What's done is done."

Gabe shook his head. "It's not that easy, Mother. Why do you think I'm the way I am? I never wanted to be so afraid of things, especially girls. I hardly ever see anyone, and when I do find someone, you tell me I'll only wind up getting hurt. No wonder why I stay to myself. But I can't do it anymore, Mother. The time is now." Gabe wiped his eyes.

"Nothing can stop you from leaving sooner or later. I must have been a fool to believe you'd stay in the first place. Of course, you can stay as long as you like." Martha grabbed some bread from the top of the refrigerator.

"You don't know how bad I feel. When I leave home, I hope to have a long career as an artist. Southwick hasn't a thing here for me, other than the factories and farms. And the both of us know I wasn't cut out for that."

She raised her eyebrows and said, "It's an honest living that many folks around here still do. So what about that new museum? Couldn't that be a starting point for you? And how about the library? They already have a few of your paintings hanging there."

"No, not in the least. You have to be dead at least fifty years to get into a museum. And as for the library, I haven't heard a thing from them since my paintings were put on display six months ago."

"I see, but aren't there other museums close by that you could show your work in?"

"You just don't get it, do you, Mother?" Gabe said, and got up. "I've had it with this town. Other than the farmlands, there's nothing but bad memories here for me. I have to leave in order to get my life on track. I'm sorry, Mother." He finished the last of his juice and left the kitchen.

He showered and felt nervous about his decision—opening a new door always had its drawbacks, he thought. He lathered up good, making sure to get all those hard-to-reach places. In his mind he could hear his mother saying, "Don't forget to get behind your ears. A boy with dirt behind his ears is a dirty boy."

###

By 7:00 P.M., Gabe was pacing back and forth at the edge of the living room.

"You must really like her," his mother said from the living room.

Gabe cracked a smile and thought just for a moment that his mother might be on his side.

"How many times do I have to tell you about girls. Do I have to mention her name for the hundredth time? Have you forgotten her already?" she said as she clicked away at the remote, shaking her head.

"Listen, Mother. Could you please leave it alone, just for one night? Didn't I just hear you say a little while ago that you don't like bringing up the past?" He glared at her.

He quickly exited the room to go get something to drink. In the kitchen, he had yet another glass of orange juice and downed it as fast as he could. If he drank as much beer as he did orange juice, he'd be an alcoholic. He wiped his mouth and looked at the clock on the wall above the kitchen sink. It was still early, but he wasn't about to wait a minute longer. He knew his mother was trying to egg him on, and if he let her, she would. *Not tonight*, Gabe thought, and walked to his room for a last look in the mirror.

His hair looked as good as it ever did, and his complexion wasn't oily as it tended to be. Feeling good, Gabe grabbed his coat, spun around, and was about to leave his room—and who but his mother was standing in his way. She had that look about her, which to Gabe meant trouble. "Listen, Mother. I'm in no mood for you tonight. Any other night I might be able to go along with your antics, but like I said, not tonight. Now will you excuse me," he said as he turned to his side so he could get out of his room. His mother followed.

"I'm just trying to help. I don't want to see you get hurt," she said in a voice that would have sounded sincere if Gabe hadn't known any better.

Gabe turned to look his mother in the eye. He knew she hated that, especially when she was lying. "You care if I get hurt. You've got to be crazy, and I'd be even crazier if I believed you." Gabe shook his head. "Listen, Mother. I'll continue this at another time," he said as he took his keys from his pocket. "Don't wait up for me," he added and stormed out of the house.

"Don't you come back tonight! And I mean it! You stay away until I say otherwise! You hear me, Gabe Arthur Chaplin?" she yelled with her head sticking out the front door. "Don't you come home tonight! I mean it!" She went on some more, but Gabe got in his car, turned up the radio, and raced out of the driveway and down the block.

###

When Gabe picked up Sara, he was still thinking about his mother. Even after they left the movie theater two hours later, she was still on his mind. But he reminded himself not to blow it this time. Sitting in the parking lot of the movie theater, Gabe didn't know if he should just take Sara home and call it a night, or stop at the diner for a bite to eat.

"I was gonna tell you this over the phone, but I wanted to talk to you in person. I had another conversation with the tall man," Gabe said and studied Sara's face.

"What is it with him. If only I could remember. Did he say what he wants?"

"No, but he keeps telling me to stay away from you as if some impending doom will occur if I don't. I wish I knew what he was talking about."

"*You* wish, what about *me*?" Sara turned away. "He is the man from my dreams. I know this has to do with the accident I was in."

"The accident? What could he possibly have to do with that?" Gabe shook his head. "Please don't hold back on me, Sara."

"Have you ever felt like you were someone else?"

Gabe shook his head. "Not that I can remember. But I've wished I was someone else plenty of times when I was young and things were bad."

She shook her head. "No, I don't mean like that. I always felt that I died in the car wreck with my mother and sister, but something breathed life back into me. The doctor, as well as my family, thinks it was just the guilt I felt over the fact that I was the only one who lived. I think Winnie believes me, but I don't even know myself. It's just so confusing." Sara sighed and bowed her head.

Gabe reached out with his hand and held hers. "Don't be so hard on yourself. If this man is after you, then something is happening. If you could only remember, or if I could just get it out of him." Gabe smiled.

"Now, don't go and do something. We don't know what we're dealing with."

Gabe raised his hands. "The next time I see him I'm gonna pick his brain. Play with him a little bit. That's all." Gabe nodded.

Sara took a deep breath. "The night is still young, so why don't you take me over to your house so I can see your paintings. You're always talking about them." Sara smiled and squirmed in her seat.

"Well, we could," he began, but cut himself off in mid-sentence. "I don't think tonight would be good. Maybe tomorrow, or some other day." Gabe looked away.

"You act as if I asked you to walk on water. I just want to see your paintings," she said and slid next to him as if suggesting more.

Gabe knew his mother would never approve of him bringing a girl into the house, no less in his room—especially after the fact that she told him not to come back tonight, which was a first for her. "I'm sorry, Sara. I think I'd better take you home," he said and started the car. She pulled away from him and sulked.

"Listen, Sara. I'd love to bring you over to see my paintings, but my mother would never approve. She's as old-fashioned as they come, and after what happened before I picked you up, I doubt that even *I* could get in the house tonight." Gabe looked away and shook his head.

"What happened?" she asked as she sat up and looked at Gabe, who headed for Route 58.

"First let me say that she doesn't approve of me seeing girls. She thinks they will screw up my life. But I know what her real reasoning is!" He looked in the rearview mirror. "What's that?" A semi, which was lit up like a Christmas tree flew by them and shook the car.

"She's afraid that if I find someone, I'll leave that much sooner, and she'll have no one to take care of her. She even said today that she knows that sooner or later I'm going to leave anyway."

"Would that be the case?"

Gabe flashed a quick glance at her. "Of course it would. I'm sick and tired of putting my life on hold because of her."

"Are you sure you really want to go?"

Gabe paused a moment and quickly said, "How can you ask such a question? I've been trying to get out from under my mother's wing since I graduated from high school. I wanted to go to a New York City art school, but she saw to it that I wouldn't. I guess I never forgave her for that."

"Is she paying for your college?"

Gabe frowned. "No, not at all. I've taken out a college loan to pay on my own. I would have gotten a job, but I have to stay home to take care of her."

"I see. Then what other reason could you have for staying, other than you want to be by your mother's side."

Gabe pulled over with a screech, jerked it into park, turned off the car, and stared at her. "Listen. I don't appreciate your badgering questions. If you don't believe me, then why don't you just come out and say it, I can handle it." Gabe pounded the steering wheel and looked away.

"I'm not badgering you in the least. I'm just trying to find out what's going on here. Listen, I know about emotions and I can see them pouring out of you like beads of sweat on a hot summer day. When it comes down to it, your relationship with your mother is all you have. Well not for long, at least on your end—that is, if you let me in, Gabe. That's the only way I'll know for sure what's going on."

"You've hit the nail right on the head, Sara. That's why it hurts so much." He cleared his throat. "Do you mind if we step out of the car. I could use the fresh air."

"Sure, why not," Sara said, and they both got out.

A million points of light filled the night sky. Gabe looked for the moon, but it was nowhere in sight. "I've never felt so mixed up in all my life," he said and continued to look toward the sky. A gust of wind blew his hair. "A few days ago I found my parents' divorce papers downstairs. I started to read them. but when I came upon the part about how my father used to beat my mother, I put them back. I just couldn't finish it," he said and kicked at the ground. "In fact, I wish I had never found the damn papers."

"That's horrible. I'm so sorry."

Gabe looked away and said, "Thanks, but there's more. I don't remember my father beating my mother." He stared at Sara, who did not move. "I asked my mother if he used to beat me, and she said he did. But I don't remember that either."

"We all forget things which are too painful to remember," Sara said and took a deep breath.

"There's just so much to decide. I just wish it were easier."

Sara gazed back at him. "What you say is true, but there's one good thing about making decisions."

"What's that?"

"You'll never have to worry that you should have done something you didn't do. When my time comes, I don't want to have any regrets. Life is too short."

Gabe shook his head. "God, you sure know what to say. How have you managed to gain such insight to life?" he asked and looked over at her. "You have the wisdom of a fifty-year-old."

"Are you trying to say that I act older than I really am?" she said and smiled.

"You could say that," Gabe said. He walked back to the car and leaned on it. Sara followed and stood next to him. "Can you just smell it—there's nothing like the sweet air of Southwick." Gabe inhaled as if smelling perfume for the first time.

Sara inhaled too. "It's beautiful. I have cornfields by my house, and at night I smell them too." Sara smiled. "You know, when my mother and sister died, it changed the way I looked at life. I'd give anything to have them both alive again."

"That must have been hard on you," Gabe said, forgetting about his own problems for a moment.

"It was," she said, and turned so that she was facing Gabe. "Though my grandmother, Winnie, made it so much easier for me. She's like a second mother."

"How did your father deal with it?"

She shook her head. "Not too well. You know, he hasn't seen another woman since. At first, I was glad—I didn't want him with another woman. But as the years passed, I let go of such feelings. But my father hasn't been able to. You can see the pain is still there. I tell him all the time that he should at least go out on a few dates. You never know. But he's too thick."

Gabe chuckled, but Sara looked at him and wasn't smiling. He cleared his throat and said, "I'm not laughing at you, Sara. It's just that my mother hasn't really loved another man since the divorce. The real reason why she doesn't want me to fall in love is so that I'll stay home and take care of her."

"Now I see why she doesn't want you to leave. Have you talked to her about this?"

Now Gabe laughed hard. "Are you kidding? I've spoken to her about it no less than a million times. The only time she changed was when she was given that medicine that led to her fainting and hitting her head, but the doctor said she can no longer take it. And, you know, when I found out, I was happy. I'd have done anything to get my old mother back. And now I have her. Like I said the other day, it's a double-edged sword."

"Listen, Gabe. You must break this cycle or you'll never be able to get your life together."

"It's hard. I was never one to make decisions, and as long as I had my mother to take care of, I had a solid excuse to leave my life the way it was. I wonder how many situations I missed living like this. I guess I'm just scared to go out on my own and take a chance."

"Have you spoken to anyone about this?"

"You mean a therapist?" Gabe said and pushed himself off the car and laughed.

"Well, something like that. I had many therapy sessions after my mother and sister died," Sara said, and moved away from the car.

"Well, I haven't. Well, not yet anyway."

"Like I said before, ever since the accident, it felt like I was another person living in someone else's body. I may look like Sara Livingston on the outside, but I don't feel like her on the inside—if that makes any sense. I also started to get many vivid dreams and waking visions of other lives—places I haven't been to before—places in foreign countries—places I saw through the haze of memories. When I started on the medication my therapists prescribed for me, I stopped having those kinds of dreams and visions. But since I met you, they started to come back." Sara's face flushed red.

"And the tall man?"

"Yes, and the tall man. I still don't remember what he represents, but I feel it's bad. I remember the first time I was aware of what was happening to me. I was at home, looking in the bathroom mirror, and I saw reflections of many faces. I closed my eyes hoping it would all disappear, but when I opened them, the same faces were there, staring back at me. Sometimes I don't even believe myself. It's all just so confusing. That's why I went to therapy in the first place. But that didn't help either. I guess I am what I am."

"And what's that?"

"I just don't know, Gabe. I don't think I should have told you any of this. It will only make things worse." Sara shook her head and turned away.

Gabe walked up to her and put his arms around her. The wind blew hard. Without thinking, he moved up to kiss her. Time seemed to stand still, as if they were the only people left in the world. Gabe felt as if his body were weightless. He never wanted to let go of that moment or Sara, for that matter.

"Why don't we go in the car," Sara said and smiled.

Gabe's heart thumped and his body tingled.

Five minutes later, the car windows steamed. Gabe was ready to burst, but then he heard his mother's voice lecturing him about having sex. Her voice seemed distant like stars, but oh so close. Gabe did his best to ignore it, but it was useless. He pulled away.

"What's wrong?" Sara asked and stared at him.

"Nothing," Gabe whispered shakily. Sara buttoned her shirt. "I'm sorry, Sara. I don't think I'm ready for this."

"Could you please just take me home," Sara said and looked away. Gabe started the car and figured once again that this was the end of the line for Sara and himself.

The ride back to Sara's house was a quiet one. Gabe rolled down the window to let the wind hit his face. Sara didn't say a word. Gabe couldn't believe how such a good night could have turned sour so quickly. "Sara, this has nothing to do with you. I'm just not ready for this," he said as he gripped the wheel, making his knuckles white.

"If you weren't ready for this, you shouldn't have taken me out. What do you expect? You know how we feel about each other. It's your mother, isn't it? I know it is," she said and looked at him.

Gabe shook his head. "I've thought about what she would say, but not this time. This time it's me. I've never been with a woman before." Gabe swallowed hard.

Sara beamed. "That's nothing to be ashamed of. In fact, it's quite noble. But I still think you need to get away from your mother for a little while. The hold she's got on you is a powerful one, and if you don't break away now, you never will."

"I can't do that now. She needs me," Gabe said and stopped for a red light.

"There you go again, making excuses," Sara said, and grabbed him by the shoulder. "You've got to take control of your own life, and distancing yourself from your mother is the first step in that direction. I'm not saying that you should forget about her, just give yourself some room."

The light changed to green, and Gabe pushed down hard on the accelerator, screeching the tires.

"You make it sound so easy, but it's not. I've lived my life like this for so long that I don't know how to be any other way. You don't know how frustrating it is," he said, pounding the steering wheel.

Sara shook her head. "You've got to start somewhere."

Gabe pulled into Sara's driveway and put the car in park. "I'm sorry for the rotten night, Sara. Believe me, I didn't plan it that way," he said and looked at her.

"I know you didn't, Gabe." She leaned over and kissed him.

"You know, you're really special. Meeting you was the best thing to happen to me in a long while. I'll call you tomorrow, and thanks," Gabe said and kissed her again. Sara smiled, got out of the car, and ran up to the front door.

CHAPTER NINE

A semi roared by with its deafening horn and plucked Gabe from a restless sleep the next morning. He glanced at his watch. "Six thirty," he mumbled.

The last thing he remembered the night before was pulling over to the side of the road on the way home. He rubbed his eyes, yawned and stretched, and looked at the rising sun. The sky was a blend of pumpkin orange and a cold steel blue gray. Birds sang and flew about, and a string of trucks, semi as well as flatbed, moved along Route 58 like angry beasts. It was just as well—Gabe had to get home.

While Gabe drove back, bits and pieces of dreams from the night before came to mind. Most of the images he remembered didn't seem to make sense—disjointed events like a newsreel spliced together from different stories. Gabe didn't know what to expect when he got home. His mother could still be mad as a rabid dog or happy as a child who just found his long lost blankie. When he pulled into the driveway, he knew he should have come home sooner.

Stiff as a tombstone, Gabe slowly got out of his car. He looked toward his house, yawned, and stretched for a second time. Every step filled his body with a burning ache. On the stoop, he grabbed the front door knob and turned, but it was locked. Shaking his head, he reached in his pocket for the keys, unlocked both locks, and wasn't surprised that the chain inside was latched.

Gabe pounded the door. "Mother!" he said. "You open up. Do you hear me? I don't want to have to break it down." He waited for her reply, but there wasn't one. *She has to be in the house*, he thought. "The side window, that's it."

Over the years, Gabe had locked himself out of the house, and he always had a backup: the window in the bathroom. The bathroom window was so destroyed from water that the lock did not work any more, so it was easy to get in.

Gabe hustled around to the side of the house. He pulled the rotted picnic bench over to the window and stood on top of it. He was still a foot away and had to reach for the ledge, but it was unlocked, as he had expected. When Gabe started to push his body through the window, he hit something and heard a loud crashing sound.

"What the hell was that?" He pulled the rest of his body through the small window and fell on the plants, breaking them even more. Getting out, he slipped on the wet dirt, fell, and banged his knee on the side of the tub. He stood there and rubbed the pain away for a good ten seconds, only to look up and see his mother standing in the doorway. "You sure can be as sneaky as a snake when you want to be," Gabe said.

"I should have known you'd come through the window," his mother said with a half smirk.

"Don't give me that, Mother." Gabe wiped the dirt off his clothes. His pants were so soiled that he needed water from the tap to clean them. He ran some hot water and wet a washcloth to try to dab the stains away. "That was a mean trick you played on me," Gabe said, and put one leg up on the toilet to get at the dirt better. He stared at her. "I could have gotten hurt."

Martha neither denied nor admitted chaining the door. "How was your night out?" Martha smiled.

Gabe shook his head and rinsed the dirty washcloth. "It went okay—though I did find out that Sara really cares about me, and that's a rare thing to find these days," he said and looked at his mother hard; caught in his stare, she looked away.

Gabe finished cleaning his pants, cleaned up the bathtub, and headed straight to the kitchen. He was so hungry he could eat breakfast, lunch, and dinner all in one sitting. He opened the refrigerator and stared with wide eyes. "Mother, where's all the food?" Gabe reached for the last of the jelly and a carton of milk, grabbed the bread from the top of the refrigerator, a knife from the draw, a glass from the cupboard, and headed for the kitchen table.

Gabe poured the milk and quickly drank. He sprayed a mouthful of it and wiped his lips. "What happened to the milk?" He rushed to the sink and flushed his mouth out with water.

She strolled to the table and said, "Oh, I forgot to tell you— the power went off last night and everything went bad. I threw most of it away, though I guess I forgot the milk." She picked the carton off the table and poured the rest down the sink. "I guess you're going to have to go out to the supermarket and get us some food," she said like a giddy child. Gabe's mother burped as if she had just finished stuffing herself with the biggest Thanksgiving dinner she had ever eaten.

"You can't honestly think I'm going to fall for that," Gabe said. He got up, stood face to face with her, and shook his head.

"Listen, if you don't believe me you can look at the garbage," she insisted.

"I don't doubt you've thrown out the food, but I know you filled your face before you did. You knew I was going to come home late and this was your way of getting back at me." Gabe walked back to the sink. His mouth was so dry he drank straight from the tap.

"How many times do I have to tell you not to drink from the faucet. Now, you go and use a glass," she insisted as if she had forgotten what had just happened.

"You're lucky I don't break every glass in the house," he warned her and wiped the dripping water from his lips and clenched his teeth.

Gabe walked away from her and passed through the sun rays that were shining through the open window. For a moment he looked like a ghost, encased in tiny specks of dust. "If I'm going to the supermarket, I'll need some money."

"What do you do with all the money I give you?"

"Whatever money you give me I use for food, and my school supplies. Have you looked in my room lately? Do you see any new stereos, televisions, or video games? Of course you don't." His voice rose like a police siren.

"All right, all right. Let me get my bag," she said and slowly walked away. Gabe never understood why she even bothered with one. She never went out.

A moment later she strolled in with a white pocketbook draped over her shoulder, and a black leather wallet clutched in her hand. She wet her finger and counted out a couple of bills that crackled, and handed them to him.

Gabe looked at the money and snatched it away from her. "Twenty-three dollars? You've got to be kidding. What can I possibly buy with this?"

"It's near the end of the month, and you know I'm always short around then."

"Don't give me that," Gabe said and choked the money. "I know about that stash you have. You must have a couple thousand dollars saved up, don't you?" Gabe circled his mother. "You thought I didn't know, didn't you." A joyless grin spread across his face. "You saw how I was scraping the bottom, and you did this to me. You know I never took a red cent from you. I don't want your money anyway!" He threw his hands in the air, the crisp bills floated to the floor. "You can keep your goddamn money!" he went on, overwhelmed with rage.

Martha shivered and took a few deep breaths. "Listen, don't act like that," she said, purring like a kitten. "I'm saving that money in the closet for the day when I'll have to go it alone."

Gabe sat down on the arm of the kitchen chair, catching his breath, and letting his anger thin out. "I'm sorry, Mother," he said, and picked up the money and put it in his pocket. "I don't know what came over me."

"Don't you worry another second. I'll fetch you some more money," Martha said with a smile.

"Mother," Gabe protested, but to no avail.

"You just let me get you some more," she yelled from her bedroom.

Martha came back with two fifties and handed them to Gabe. "One is for shopping, and the other you can do with as you please." She smiled.

Gabe stood up, his mouth wide open. This was a first for his mother. "Thanks, Mother," he said, ready to leave. He turned around. "Is there anything special you need?"

She pulled out a list and handed it to him. "You don't have to get everything, but please try, especially the eggs. You know I can't go without my eggs in the morning," she said and smiled.

Still shocked, Gabe got into his car and headed for the supermarket.

###

Gabe arrived home an hour later and stocked the shelves with the groceries he had just bought. He wanted to surprise his mother. Normally, they had a deal that Gabe would go and get the stuff and his mother would put it away—what she could reach, that was. Gabe even bought a thick steak he hoped his mother would cook. He folded the brown bags and neatly put them away too.

"Mother," Gabe said and walked through the house. "Mother," he said again and poked his head down the basement door to see if she was there. But again there was no answer.

Standing in the kitchen, he heard the sound of metal hitting stone. *It can't be*, he thought. He went out the side door and into the backyard. He quickly scanned the yard, and sure enough, he could see a head covered in a red silk scarf, slowly moving up and down. He couldn't believe that she would already be out and about since she had only gotten out of the hospital a few days ago, and especially since she wasn't taking her medication anymore.

"Mother?" he said and trotted over to her. "Mother, what are you doing out here?"

She kept digging away, not aware that Gabe was calling. The hard-hitting wind didn't help. "Mother?" Gabe said, only this time he was standing behind her. He could see that she was weeding the garden. She turned around.

"Gabe, you're already back," she said and glanced at her wrist, but she had taken her watch off before she came outside. "What time is it?" she said and fought with the wind to keep her scarf from blowing off.

"It's about twelve thirty. Are you coming in?" he asked, his hair blowing in his face.

"Yeah, I think so. I'm not used to being outdoors." She slowly stood.

"Would you please hold this for me?" she asked. Gabe took a small hand rake from her. He could see that she was sweating profusely.

"Shouldn't you be inside, resting?"

"No, not in the least. The doctor said I should go outdoors more often. He said a little sun would be good for my health, as well as any exercise I can get."

"Haven't I told you that a thousand times. Since when are you one for listening?" He rolled his eyes and smiled.

By the time Martha walked back to the house, which was only fifty or so feet away, she was so worn out she nearly collapsed on the kitchen floor. "I need some tea," she said, and started to walk over to the stove. Gabe grabbed her by the elbow and helped her to sit down.

"You just sit back, and let me take care of you," he insisted. He made some tea for her and put her to sleep.

He went to his room to paint, and only stopped when his stomach growled. When he looked at the clock on the wall, he realized he'd been painting for four hours. He quickly washed up, had a bite to eat, and headed over to the museum.

###

The parking lot was again filled, so he parked on the grass across the street. Outside of his car, he scanned the open land that surrounded the museum and realized that all the farms in Southwick would soon be gone—that would be true especially after the museum would take root. He could imagine that many other buildings would follow, and then soon all the open land would disappear. He liked Southwick the way it was—wide and open. He smiled wistfully.

Inside the museum, he asked for Sara and was told she was working in the Modern section today.

He spotted her at the information booth talking to a short gray-haired woman. Walking toward her, he passed a mother and her two children, what looked to be an art class, a group of senior citizens, and a couple of farmers wearing their trademark overalls and straw hats. Gabe thought, *It's nice to see all these different people in the same place enjoying the same things.* He smiled.

Gabe walked up behind Sara and called her name.

She smiled with eyes wide. "Gabe, it's so nice to see you," she said over the drone of people whispering and walking by. She waved him closer, and stared. "I have something to tell you." She looked away and took a deep breath. "It's just so hard," Sara said and looked at her watch.

"What's so hard?"

Sara shook her head. "I get a break in fifteen minutes. Why don't we meet at the cafe, and I'll tell you then," she said. Her eyes sparkled with life.

Gabe stared back. "What is it, Sara?"

She took another deep breath and waved her hand. "I promise, Gabe, I'll tell you later."

"Okay." Gabe shook his head.

"Don't wait on the long lines—just go toward the back by the bathrooms, and I'll meet you there," she said, smiled, and left.

Gabe followed her as far as he could see. A queasy feeling grew in his stomach, which he knew wasn't from nausea but from excitement over seeing her again. Gabe looked at a few more paintings and wondered if his work would ever be in a museum. With that in mind, he smiled and headed for the cafe to meet Sara.

He waited in the back like she had said, but she didn't come. Gabe wasn't an impatient person by nature, but he did start to get antsy when twenty-five minutes had passed and she still didn't show up. Gabe headed over to the soda machine and bought one for himself. He quickly returned to the back of the cafe and again waited for Sara. Five minutes later, she finally showed up. Her face was flushed as if she had been crying. Gabe put down his soda and rushed over to meet her. "Sara, what's wrong?"

Sara cried and put her arms around him. Gabe hugged her back as she continued to sob. She was trying to speak, but her words were lost in her muffled sobs. Gabe pulled away and again asked, "What's wrong?" his eyes wide open.

"It's Winnie. She has chest pains," Sara managed to say in between gasps of air. "They took her to Southwick General. Do you think you could take me there?" she asked, and wiped her eyes and face with the sleeve of her shirt.

"Sure, I can take you."

Sara sniffled and wiped her nose. "I just have to let my supervisor know, and then we can leave. I'll meet you out front," Sara said and left.

Gabe stood there for a moment, and it seemed that not a single soul saw what had just transpired. Everyone was too engrossed in their own business to notice, except the tall man, who seemed to notice everything that concerned Sara.

Outside the museum, Gabe glared at the tall man who stood inside the front doors. *Who the hell is this guy, and what does he really want?* Gabe thought with a shake of his head. A vicious wind from nowhere blew Gabe's hair in his face. The sky turned darker.

CHAPTER TEN

The car ride to the hospital was so quiet it was deafening. Sara had finally stopped crying, but her eyes were bloodshot, and her cheeks rosy. Gabe drove at a good speed, not too much over the limit of forty five, but Sara didn't seem to mind. It was as if she hoped the ride would take forever. There was always the chance that Winnie might be dead by the time they got there.

Finally, not able to take the silence any longer, Gabe spoke. "Has something like this ever happened to your grandmother before?" He eased on the pedal for a red light.

"Last summer she collapsed at a picnic, but it was just heat stroke, and other than getting a seasonal cold, nothing bad has happened to her. She's the sweetest woman in the world, and I don't know what I'd do without her," Sara said, and looked like she was going to cry again.

The winds were blowing madly as they swept through Southwick. Gabe's car swayed back and forth from the force. The sky was now black and ominous, and rain poured out as if a million people had just started to cry. Even with the wipers on high, Gabe still had a problem seeing. He flipped on the lights and hoped they wouldn't have to pull over. Then the windows inside started to fog because of the many leaks his old car had. He flipped on the defogger, and in no time, he was able to see again. Ten minutes later they pulled into the hospital parking lot.

"I'll drop you off here and find a spot," Gabe said and stopped right in front of the hospital's main entrance. "I'll be right with you." Sara got out of the car and quickly headed for the lobby.

Gabe drove away, circling the lot for that one precious spot everyone had missed. But there were no spots close to the hospital. Gabe found the nearest one and parked.

It wasn't that far away, and on any normal day it would have been a short walk, but by the time he hopped the curb and rushed to the lobby, he was soaked. The electric doors slid open, and Gabe walked in. They too were fogged up. He took a few seconds to catch his breath while he looked for Sara. He quickly spotted her at the information booth. Her turn had just come. Dripping wet, Gabe ran to her.

"I told you I don't know when she was brought in, but it couldn't have been more than an hour ago. Will you please just look up the name. It's spelled, W-I-N-I-F-R-E-D E-A-S-T-M-A-N!" Sara shook her head.

The receptionist with a bushy head of platinum blond hair quickly typed in Winnie's name, waited a moment, and then looked up. "It says that she was brought into the emergency room about forty-five minutes ago. Let me see if she's been admitted yet." She looked down at her monitor.

"Can I go and see her?" Sara asked as Gabe put his arm on her shoulder. Sara turned and looked at him.

"I'll have to make a call first to check." Sara turned back and fidgeted while the woman made the call.

"Sara, now take it easy. I'm sure your grandmother is in good hands. Why don't you go and get a drink," Gabe suggested, pointing to the water fountain nearby. "I'll handle the rest," he assured her.

Sara's face was still flushed, and her blue eyes were now nothing but a dark cloudy sky.

When the receptionist looked up, Sara was gone. "Do you know where that girl with the blue eyes disappeared to?"

"She went for some water," Gabe said.

"Are you also family?"

He shook his head. "No, I'm not. I'm just a friend."

"Well, only immediate family can visit her at this time."

Gabe leaned over the counter and asked, "How is she?"

She hesitated slightly. "I don't know."

"What room is she in?" Gabe asked and looked right through her.

"It looks like she's still in the emergency room. Do you know where that is?"

"Yes," Gabe answered. "Unfortunately I do," he shook his head, and quickly ran over to tell Sara where her grandmother was.

Sara's eyes were puffy and red. Gabe didn't want to alarm her, but he had to tell her. "She hasn't been admitted yet, so they're keeping her in the emergency room." He sat down next to her and held her hand.

Together they walked to the emergency room and were let in. The moment Sara saw her grandmother with all those tubes and wires sticking out of her, she became hysterical and had to be led away by a nurse. She asked Sara first if she'd ever had a sedative before and if she was going to drive in the next few hours. When Sara answered yes to the first question and no to the second, the nurse gave her a white pill and a cup of water. Sara eagerly swallowed the pill, as if it would take away her sadness.

Gabe gently stroked Sara's hair while they sat in the waiting room. The pill was already taking effect. Sara was still awake but calm as a glass of water.

Gabe watched a man who had blood all over his shirt walk into the emergency room. The man begged to be admitted, but the receptionist wanted the basic information first. He kept saying he was going to die if he didn't see a doctor. He finally gave in and said what he had to, only to wait just like the others. Sara's head fell onto Gabe's shoulder but quickly snapped back and fell to the other side.

Gabe was surprised to see that Sara's family wasn't there yet. *Maybe they don't even know*, he thought.

###

By the time Sara's family did arrive, Sara was asleep, but Gabe was wide awake. The bright fluorescent lights above didn't help any, and neither did the loud television on the wall that was playing the Clint Eastwood spaghetti western, *High Plains Drifter*. Seeing that Sara's family had finally arrived, Gabe nudged her a few times to get her attention. "Sara, your family's here." He nudged her a second time.

Sara opened her eyes and blinked a few times until they adjusted to the bright lights. "How long was I asleep?" she asked, stretched, and yawned.

Gabe looked at the clock on the wall and said, "I think for about forty minutes. Could be longer. Why don't we go and talk with your family. I'm sure they're as worried as we are."

Sara finished yawning, got up and said, "You stay here and let me talk to them. They're going to be nothing but nerves."

"Are you sure you're going to be okay?" Gabe said and stood.

"I'll be all right. And thanks, Gabe, I really appreciate what you're doing for me," Sara said and smiled. Gabe smiled back, feeling as warm as a campfire. He glanced at the television to see the famous scene where Clint Eastwood pulls aside his poncho, revealing the piece of metal beneath. *Too bad life wasn't that easy*, he thought.

Sara walked over to her family.

"Does she have a room yet?" her father asked.

"As of about an hour ago she didn't. So why don't you guys go and have a seat and I'll find out what's going on," Sara said, trying to handle the situation. "Do you remember Gabe?" she said and pointed in his direction. "He's sitting over there. Why don't you go and have a seat with him. I'm sure he'd like the company."

Sara walked to the desk and asked about Winnie. This time there was a different woman sitting behind the counter. Sara waited patiently while the woman looked up Winnie's name on her computer. "I'm sorry, but I don't see the name," the plump woman said as she looked back at her screen, chewing up the end of her pen.

"Listen, my grandmother was in the emergency room less than an hour ago. Now could you please just tell me where she is? My family and I would like to see her," Sara insisted.

The plump woman shrugged her shoulders. "Okay, okay, I'll go and see if your grandmother is still in the emergency room." The receptionist got up and added, "Now, don't you go and tell everyone here that I left the room, or I'll be so busy seeing if all the other patients are all right that I won't be able to do my job." She flashed a smile before she left.

Sara would have laughed any other time as the plump woman left. Sara looked around and could see that the waiting area was just about empty, except for a man and a woman who looked to be half asleep. A mother and two small children, and an old man who had dried blood on his face and who looked like he'd had too much to drink also occupied the lobby. In less than a minute, the woman with the chewed-up pen came back. She went through the back door and sat down in front of her computer.

"I checked with the floor nurse, and she said your grandmother was taken to a room about ten minutes ago. That's why it wasn't on my computer yet. I don't know the number, so you're going to have to check with admissions in the main building."

"Thanks." Sara turned and left.

At that moment, the doors burst open with two stretchers. The smell of burning flesh filled the air. Sara backed away, covering her mouth. Her eyes widened. Gabe couldn't see the bodies, but he knew something was wrong by Sara's actions. *It's Winnie*, he thought and got up and rushed over to her side just in time to catch her from falling. His nose tingled, and he wiped it.

"Are you all right?" Gabe just happened to look up and saw what she already had seen. He looked away and held on to her. "Let's get out of here." He quickly led Sara away and walked over to her family. Gabe was still shaking his head, and rubbing his nose.

"How's Winnie doing?" Jenna asked as she reached for her sister's hand and clenched her brown bear with the other.

"I don't know, but she's been given a room. We have to go to admissions in the main building to find out which one." Sara tried to smile.

Ralph stood silent, his face a ghostly white. Sara's father stood on the outskirts of this whole affair. He looked more like an observer than an actual participant. Seeing Ralph was outside the group, Johnny walked over to him and put his arm around his shoulder. "Come on, Dad, she'll be all right," Johnny said, trying to console him.

Ralph turned to him and gave him a look so penetrating that his eyes shot open, and he took a step back. "Can you guarantee that she'll be all right?" Ralph asked, his eyes holding Johnny's.

Johnny rolled his eyes. "Of course I can't. You know that. Let's just go, Dad," he said and turned to find the others.

The Livingston family and Gabe walked over to the main building and found out that Winnie was staying in the east wing in room 228. The newly renovated wing had all the latest modern features, from computerized patient beds that monitored their every bodily function, to the top-of-the-line laser surgery equipment.

They all rode the elevator up to the second floor. Jenna closed her eyes and gripped her bear, which Sara had given her last Christmas, that much more.

The elevator stopped with a jerk. Jenna opened her eyes and said, "When are we going to see Winnie?" The doors slid open, and the smell of disinfectant mixed with what smelled like chicken soup filled Sara's nose.

Sara bent down and lightly held her sister by the shoulders. "We're going to see Winnie in a few minutes. Now, you're going to have to be on your best behavior. Winnie isn't feeling well right now and needs all the smiles she can get." Sara kissed her sister on the forehead. Jenna smiled as Sara stood up and walked over to the nearest room to see which direction they had to go. "This way, everybody," she said as she waved them over.

Doctors carrying clipboards walked by. Nurses with pills in cups hurried to rooms. Ward personnel dressed in white were busy preparing the next available room for new patients. A constant paging of doctors on the overhead speakers screamed to be heard. It was complete organized chaos in motion.

When the group approached the room, a candy striper, who didn't look a day over eighteen, greeted them. Her blond hair was pulled up and clipped in a tight neat bun. Her long white-and-red striped skirt had brown stains on the front, and she wore thin gold glasses at the tip of her long nose.

"We're here to see Winnie Eastman, I mean Winifred Eastman. She is in this room, isn't she?" Sara asked. Her eyes fluttered, and she rubbed her right temple.

"Yes, she is. She's in the bed closest to the window. She was just brought in no more than twenty minutes ago. Her sheets were still warm from the laundry when they put her in. She's a sweet woman," the candy striper said with a smile.

"Is she going to be all right?"

The candy striper smiled at Sara and said, "I'd love to say yes, but not all of her tests are in yet—though she is conscious and in good spirits. Why don't you go and see her."

Sara looked at Ralph and he waved for her to go. Slowly she walked into the room. Jenna started to follow, but her father put out his arm. "Let Sara go first, dear." He looked down at Jenna.

Sara passed by an empty bed to her right, a chair, and a white ruffled curtain that was drawn halfway to separate the two beds. She glanced at the window and could see that it was still raining and that the cloudy gray sky had turned dark as a pupil. The few steps to her grandmother's bedside seemed like a hundred—time a replay stuck in motion. Sara studied her grandmother's features—she hadn't realized until now how small her nose was, and that there was a tiny bump on the bridge of it. She took a few steps back and grabbed the chair she had just passed. She pulled it up next to her grandmother's bed, trying not to wake her, but she was a light sleeper. Winnie's eyes opened and slowly fluttered, adjusting to the bright lights. She looked to her left and saw Sara sitting there. She smiled, raised her arm slightly, and wiggled her fingers. Sara reached over and playfully touched her wrinkled, bony hand.

The rest of the family and Gabe waited in the background, motionless.

"Winnie?" Sara said as if she were out of breath. "How are you feeling?" she asked and rubbed her eyes.

"I'm okay, young lady. Now, don't you worry about me, I'll be fine. I can't believe how much you look like your mother. You know, when your mother was five years old she used to threaten to run away from home some day if we didn't leave her alone. She was unbearable at times, especially when someone would tell her what to do. Anyway, one day your mother said that she was going to leave—run away from home. She packed a small bag with lunch, and her favorite stuffed animal, which was this old beat-up bear her father had won at a street carnival two summers before. Since she kept warning us that she was going to leave for good, we didn't pay her any attention the day she packed that bag. Then there was this knock at the door. And do you know who was at the door, knocking?" A big grin spread across her face.

"My mother." Sara smiled.

"That's right, your mother. She was standing there with the sun at her back, and her little care package draped over her shoulder. She just stood there for a moment and finally did say something. She asked me which way to go. Can you believe that?" Winnie said, smiling from ear to ear. Sara was smiling too. "I want you to promise me one thing. You have to promise you'll never run away from us. You mean too much to me, and it would just break my heart. And we both know what a broken heart feels like, don't we." She kissed Sara softly on the forehead and stroked her hair. "You sure do have your mother's looks."

"Thanks, Winnie. I would never leave you or the family." Sara wiped the corner of her eye.

"Speaking of the family, where are they? I bet Ralph is worried sick," she said and smiled.

"They're all just outside the room. Do you want me to bring them in?" Sara asked, and rose.

"Sure, bring them all in," Winnie said and sat up in bed. Sara got up and adjusted her pillow.

There was no need for Sara to get her family. They walked in a moment after Winnie asked for them.

Jenna stood at the foot of the bed, Ralph by the window, and Gabe and Johnny at Sara's side.

"I'm glad you're all here, especially you, little Jenna. Now come over here and give Winnie a big kiss," she said and parted her arms like Jesus.

Little Jenna, with her long bouncing pigtails, rushed over to give Winnie a kiss. She pulled away and said, "Are you going to be all right?" Her green eyes were glassy and bloodshot.

"Of course I am," Winnie replied and shook her head. She gave Sara and the rest of them a quick look, but the blank expressions on their faces told her they knew about as much as she did. She took a deep breath.

Standing there, Gabe felt like an outsider. He studied all their faces, especially Sara's, who looked on the verge of crying. He looked down and saw that Ralph's right hand was shaking, and saw worry in Sara's father's wide hazel eyes. Jenna was holding her bear, but she seemed the least shaken.

Ralph walked over to the bed, looked down at Winnie, and said, "You better not take a vacation. We still have a lot of living left to do." He bent down and kissed his wife on the forehead. His striking eyes were now dull and lifeless.

Winnie smiled and said, "I'll be fine, Ralph."

A nurse, wide as a twin garage, strolled in. She had cherry red lips, curly eyelashes that were thick like a forest, and a voice so soft it seemed to float down from heaven.

"Mrs. Eastman, how are we doing today?" the nurse asked. She stood with a pill in one hand and a cup of water in the other. "I see we have visitors." She smiled. "This large pill is for the pain in your head. It would have come sooner, but I had to okay it with the doctor. You know how they can be," she said as she handed the cup of water and the pill to Winnie. "You take this and just sit back," the nurse added.

Winnie took the pill and swallowed hard. "Anything to get rid of the pain in my head," she said and downed the rest of the water as a chaser.

The nurse turned away from Winnie. "I'd only give her another five minutes." She turned back to Winnie and took the empty cup from her hand. "You're going to be sleeping like a baby before you can say 'hospital bed.' Is there anything I could do for you before I go, Mrs. Eastman?"

"No, but if I need anything, I'll give you a buzz," Winnie assured her. The nurse smiled and left.

"Sara, I think we'd better get going now and let Winnie get some rest," her father said and leaned over the bed. "You take care, Mom, and don't hesitate to give us a call. We'll set up the television," he said and pointed to the one on the wall, "If you'd like us to, that is."

"Yes, that would be just fine," Winnie said as her eyes started to close. With a wave of her hand, Winnie motioned Sara's father to come closer. "John," she said in a whisper, "take care of Sara. Stay close to her and always go that extra mile for her. She's one special girl." He shook his head, kissed her on the cheek, and moved away.

One by one, they all said goodbye—even Gabe got in on the action and kissed Winnie on the cheek. Sara looked at him and smiled.

###

Sara drove with Gabe, while the rest of her family went home in her father's car.

"Can you believe that?" Sara said while Gabe started the car. "Not one of them knew a thing. I find that hard to believe," she went on as Gabe drove out of the parking lot.

"Listen, Sara. It takes time for tests to be completed. The moment they find out anything, I'm sure they'll inform you."

"I guess you're right." Sara squirmed in her seat. "But the waiting is killing me."

"Sara, these people deal with these kinds of things every day of their lives. They see good and bad come their way, and believe me, it doesn't effect them like it would you or me."

Gabe looked over at Sara and saw tears in her eyes. She turned away, but soon she was sucking air as if she was out of breath. Her tears continued to fall and didn't seem like they would ever stop.

###

Gabe stopped at the diner for a bite to eat, and about forty-five minutes later, pulled into Sara's driveway.

"Could you back the car out?" She looked at the front of her house, which was lit up from a bright porch light.

"Sure." He parked the car on the street.

He scooted over next to her and put his arm around her shoulder. Now that the rain finally stopped, Sara rolled down the window and breathed in the moist air.

"You know, I can remember the many summer nights when my mother used to take me out back and show me the stars. She knew exactly where they were at various times of the year. She also knew where the planets were too. The night we saw the shooting star couldn't have been more than a few days before she died. You should have seen it move across the sky," she said and raised her hand to show Gabe just how it happened. "It moved in an arch with alarming speed. You know, my mother never saw a shooting star before that day. She said it was her lucky star. After she died, it was months before I looked at the sky again. Then, one night I heard this noise coming from our back yard, and who but Winnie was out there, tripping over her feet in the dark. 'What are you doing out here, Winnie?' I asked, barely able to conceal my laughter. 'I'm trying to catch a glimpse of the planets,' she answered and looked toward the night sky."

Gabe was now laughing too.

"I know that some day we all have to go, but I'm not ready for Winnie to leave just yet, but I feel her time is up."

Gabe pulled away for a moment and said, "How could you possibly know that?"

"I could tell by the way they looked at us, and the fact that they didn't come out and tell me what happened to her. Why else would they act that way?" Sara rubbed her eyes.

"First of all, these people have a million and one things on their mind. And like I said before, if they knew what was wrong with Winnie, I'm sure they would have told you. It's their job to."

"It doesn't matter, Gabe. If she lives today, sooner or later the hand of death will snatch her life away. It's as simple as that. It will happen to all of us. Well, at least most of us."

"Listen, Sara, it's getting late and my mother is going to wonder where I am," Gabe said and reached for his keys.

She put out her hand and touched his forearm. "Don't leave. Well, at least not yet. I don't want to be alone, and the rest of my family is probably sleeping, except for my father, who I'd bet is sitting in front of the TV with a can of beer and the paper. Please don't leave just yet." Sara gazed at Gabe.

He shook his head. "I just don't know, Sara. I could come over tomorrow as early as you'd like, but I still have a lot of work to do tonight."

"Listen, I've got something to show you. I hope you're not afraid of the water. Come on, let's go," she said and got out of the car.

Gabe was tired, hungry, and just wanted to go home, but all of a sudden, Sara was full of life and bursting with energy.

"Come on," she said and stood in the street, waiting for Gabe. "Come on," she said again and waved her hand.

It was as if something had taken over her mind, body, and soul. Sara laughed as she spun in front of her house.

Watching her, Gabe shook his head, and got out of his car to try to calm her down, and heard a single crow. He craned his neck and saw them perched on the wire, still, as if they were stuffed. Gabe stared hard, but the crows still did not move.

He turned, looked at Sara, and said, "Okay, okay. I'll come." He slammed the door, causing the birds to caw and fly away. He followed Sara who already had a good lead on him. Though he couldn't see her, he followed her voice, which rang out in the quiet night.

"What are we doing, Sara?" Gabe asked and stuck close to her. "Where are you taking me?" He went on huffing and puffing. She laughed. If Gabe didn't know any better, he'd swear she was on drugs.

Along the way to wherever Sara was taking him, Gabe thought back to the night he had taken Sara to the windmill. With the shoe now on the other foot, he realized he didn't like it.

They quickly passed her father's shed, a dozen or so thirty-foot Poplars, and green forsythia on either side of a narrow dirt path.

"Come on, Gabe. We're almost there," Sara said and stopped to look behind her.

Gabe was starting to get frustrated. Forsythia whipped his arms and legs. "This is crazy, Sara. What are we doing out here in the dark?" Sara stood in the path and waited until Gabe finally caught up. Gabe stopped in front of her with his hands at his side, chest heaving. With a three-quarter moon hanging in the sky, they could see each other's faces, though there wasn't enough light out to read a book.

"Every time I feel the way I do, I come down here to have a swim. I hope you like the water," she said and ran away from him, laughing and discarding every bit of clothing she had on.

Moments later, he heard a loud splash. "It's not cold at all!" she shouted.

Gabe still stood in the same spot. He had never seen a girl disrobe in front of him, except for his last girlfriend, which turned out to be a disaster, and the models he drew in figure drawing class—but that was different. Normally Gabe would have stayed put, but tonight was anything but normal. Hearing Sara's playfulness, Gabe decided he'd join her. He took everything off but his underwear, leaving his clothes in a neat pile on the ground. Gaining courage by the second, he now followed the dirt path down to the moonlight-rippled water.

Sara waited and encouraged him to jump in with a shout of, "You'll love it! It's great!" Suddenly, Gabe paused at the edge of the lake as if an invisible hand were tugging him from behind.

"Well, just don't stand there. Jump in," she said and playfully giggled and splashed some more water.

"It better not be cold."

He slowly turned around expecting to see his mother, but of course she wasn't there. He ran toward the lake and made the plunge, jumping as high in the air as he could. Just as he was a few inches above the water, he thought back to the day his mother caught him skinny-dipping with his last girlfriend. He remembered the humiliation of that day, and thought what an inopportune time to recall such a thing. Gabe splashed into the water and shot up.

"It's freezing in here. I thought you said it wasn't cold," Gabe said, shivering. He swam over to Sara.

"It's not that bad if you're used to it." She smiled.

"Used to it. I don't think I could ever get used to this." Gabe shivered uncontrollably. Sara playfully splashed him with water and swam away.

"Well, are you going to swim? Or are you just going to stay in one place with your teeth rattling?"

Gabe swam under water and shot out like a cork, and dunked Sara. "Now who's laughing." He let her up for some air and did it again. His nervousness was now replaced with joy and laughter. He let Sara up a second time and quickly swam away from her.

"Where do you think you're going?" she said and tried to grab his arm.

"Nowhere, just away from you," he joked and swam away with water splashing everywhere.

Gabe swam away from Sara, and by the time he looked back, she was gone. Out of sight.

After about thirty seconds, Gabe realized he was alone. He stopped swimming and said, "Sara, where are you?" He received no answer. Gabe called out again and again, and still no answer. "Sara, you'd better not be playing games with me." Gabe quickly swam about, trying to locate her.

"Gabe," she finally called out.

Gabe spun to where he thought Sara's voice was coming from. "Sara, is that you? Are you okay?" He swam in her direction.

"I'm fine, Gabe," she said and came out from the shadows so he could see her.

In the moonlight, Gabe could see Sara standing by the edge of the lake. He could see the swells of her breasts and outline of her nipples through her wet shirt. Gabe swallowed hard, looking at her standing there with a glazed look in her eyes. She smiled, and with her finger motioned for him to come to her.

"Don't you think you've had enough of that cold water," she said.

Gabe swam over to the edge of the lake and paused. "Could you get my clothes?" he asked and looked away.

"I'll keep my eyes closed, I promise," Sara said and smiled.

Gabe didn't want to make it an issue, but he didn't want Sara to see him with a tent in his underwear. As much as he wanted to have sex, he was still afraid to. He climbed out of the water, splashing as he did. He walked by Sara who had her hands over her eyes, but every so often, she'd look through them to have a look.

"I said no peeking. Have you seen my clothes and shoes? I can't seem to find them," Gabe said as he looked around.

"I'll get them, Gabe," she said and walked to the tree where she had hidden his clothes. "They're over here," she called out and bent down to pick them up.

"I'll be right there, Sara," he said nervously, and walked over to her and quickly put on his clothes.

Sara moved toward him, her exterior of calmness never changed. She held out her hand and waited for Gabe to take it. Gabe thought that he saw an expression of disappointment on Sara's face, but, as much as he cared for her, he still wasn't ready for any serious physical contact.

"As I recall, I promised to tell you something. With all that had happened before, I just plain forgot to. Why don't you follow me." She looked him in the eyes and didn't let go. Gabe followed quickly, as if she had a power over him that he couldn't resist.

"Okay."

Gabe followed her lead. *This is her territory now*, he thought.

Sara led Gabe down a dirt path, and every so often he'd step on a branch, or stub his toe on a rock. None of this seemed to trouble Sara in the least.

Gabe stepped on another rock and said, "Ouch. I hope you know where we're going. My feet are killing me."

"Don't worry, we're almost there," Sara assured him and continued to lead through a narrow man-made path.

"Almost where?"

"Remember the other night when I told you all that stuff about me?"

Gabe nodded.

"Well, after you left, I was drawn to the spot I'm taking you to. I was visited by a spirit, and talking with her put all that I've been through in a new light—call it a revelation if you like. I only wish it were sooner. Here we are," she said and stopped in front of an old, dilapidated windmill.

"Are you sure you have the right place?" Gabe looked on with wide staring eyes, as if he had expected her to show him something like the Taj Mahal.

"Yes, this is the place. Let's go inside," Sara said with her full attention toward the structure in front of them. Her eyes were now glowing like the moon, and in a trancelike state.

The windmill was falling apart, though Gabe imagined that in its prime it might have looked magnificent. The side wood panels had split and fallen off, and was gray as a storm-blown sky.

Sara entered first but paused when she passed through the large broken opening, and looked over her left shoulder. "Aren't you coming in?"

"Yeah, I'm coming," Gabe said with an impending sense of doom. *If only mother would pull me away now*, he thought. Gabe took a step forward and heard the snap of a branch, and then footsteps. He spun around. An icy chill ran up his back. He looked hard but didn't see anything.

"Well, are you coming?" Sara asked and disappeared into the

old windmill. Gabe turned back, paused one more time to have a look, and started to follow her in.

"I wouldn't do that if I were you," a baritone voice said. Gabe turned around and saw the tall man.

"What do you want with us?" Gabe clenched his fists and walked up to him.

"This is between Sara and myself. I bet you she still hasn't told you what she really is?"

"No, I haven't, fallen angel." Sara slowly walked out of the windmill.

The tall man smiled. "So you know the truth. You also must know that you cannot escape me any longer. The time is now."

"Sara, what's going on here?" Gabe froze.

"I told you she will never tell you what she really is. Why don't you tell him, tell this mortal the truth about your past." He pointed at her. "Let him decide before you do what you were about to."

"What were you gonna do to me, Sara?"

She wiped her forehead. "He's got you all confused, Gabe. Don't trust him for a second. His path leads to the darkness." She turned to the tall man and said, "I know who you really are. You're the last of the fallen angels. Your days are running out, and you want to free yourself of damnation before that happens. I am here to see that that doesn't happen." Sara sneered at him.

"How's Winnie doing? I bet she's just fine, isn't she." The tall man smiled.

Sara stared back. "What did you do to her? I swear, if you did anything to her, I will put a stop to you once and for all."

"Stop to me?" The tall man's eyes widened. "What do you think, I'm a fool?"

Gabe noticed them first. They were quiet, but soon all the trees surrounding them were filled with crows. Their black eyes were now blood red and glowing like fireflies.

"Sara, the birds," Gabe said and took a few steps backward, stumbling as he did. The tall man laughed, and Gabe's skin tickled with fear.

The crows started to squawk, but quickly their squawks rose like an orchestra building to a crescendo. Soon they filled the air, and Gabe couldn't see. "Sara," he screamed and waved his hands.

"Gabe, follow me into the windmill. He and his birds can't come in here."

"I'll be waiting for you outside," the tall man said.

"You don't have to worry about that. For the next few minutes I'll be your shadow," Gabe assured her and quickly moved his feet. "Sara, you have to tell me something. Why do all those black birds follow that guy around? It's as if he has power over them."

"They represent all the souls he's captured and destroyed."

"My God, that's a lot of people." Gabe gasped.

"It is, Gabe. It is." Sara abruptly stopped, slowly turned around and stared at Gabe. She looked at the ground, and with the heel of her shoe, drew a line in the dirt. "See the line?" she said and pointed with her foot.

Gabe moved closer and could see from the moonlight above that shone through the broken roof. "I do."

"Once you step over this line, forever will your life change."

"Sara, what are you talking about?" Gabe asked and dared not cross the line.

But then it happened as if some invisible hand had pushed him in the back.

In the blink of an eye, Gabe was over the line—then it began. His stomach started to feel like he was on a roller coaster. Then the unrecognizable voices filled his ears. He covered them and shook his head.

"Sara, what's going on?"

A cold fright made it impossible for him to move.

"Now hold on. Push a little more. The head is almost out," an excited woman's high-pitched voice said.

Moments later, they heard a baby's cry. It echoed as if they were in a cave. Flashes of bright lights came, swirling like a colorful acid trip, followed by images of Gabe's past, present, and future.

"Sara, what's going on?" Gabe asked. An icy chill stayed on his back like a wet tee shirt. "Please tell me what's going on," he said. His face was white, and his eyes wide. "Sara, please." Gabe sat down in the dirt with his head in his hands. He tried to make sense of what had just happened. Sara sat down next to him and put her arm around his sweating neck.

"Don't worry, Gabe. I felt the same way the other night. You know, you're the only person I would show this to."

Gabe looked up. "Why me? What about your family?" he asked, clearing his throat.

"I have tried, but they would never believe me. They would just tell me it's my overactive imagination dealing with the deaths of my mother and sister that's getting the best of me. But after the other night, when I found this place, everything made sense. There's more here than I am even telling you. I just don't know," Sara said and walked away from Gabe. She spun around and added, "I'm only telling you this because if something should happen, I want you to know there is a way out, but you have to come back here as soon as it happens."

"As soon as *what* happens?" Gabe asked, his skin tight.

"Don't you want to be with me forever?"

"I do."

"Well, you just took the first step in making that happen." Sara smiled.

"But I don't even fully understand what you are." Gabe looked Sara over with wide staring eyes.

"Why are you looking at me like that? You don't believe me either, do you?" Sara said and looked away. "You think I'm crazy. Now you know why I didn't tell my family and why I was afraid to tell you."

Gabe looked up and said, "No, why?"

"Sara was in the car when her mother and sister died in the accident. Not only was she there, but she also died with them two and a half years ago. I know that for sure now."

"What do you mean she died with them? How could that possibly be?" Gabe shook his head.

"I know it's confusing, but I now know that's what happened. Why, I'm not exactly sure," Sara said and patted her chest. "But I know it's for a reason. Gabe, you have to understand that the real Sara died in that car accident with her mother and sister. I remember the look my family had on their faces when I first tried to tell them—it was kind of like the look on your face now. But who could blame them, or you. I didn't want to share this with anyone. I was afraid of what it might do to them, not to mention me. But finding this place the other day put a new light on everything, including us." Sara took a deep breath and looked away.

Gabe got up and said, "That's perfectly honest, Sara. But I'm still confused about the whole thing. How could you have died when you're standing right in front of me at this very moment?"

"*Sara* died." She slammed her hands at her sides. "All I ever wanted was to be like everyone else. I never asked to be what I am. I don't even know how it happened in the first place, jumping from one body to the next." Sara pounded her fist into her open hand.

"I wish I could help you, but I don't understand what you're talking about."

Nervousness came over Gabe, starting from the bottom of his feet and traveling right up to the ends of the hair on his head. A strong wind from out of nowhere started to howl.

The windmill filled with a terrible stench like that of a hundred rotted corpses. Gabe covered his nose, and hoped to never smell it again. But Sara stood there as if it didn't bother her. Gabe started coughing up slick green chunks. Sara quickly moved away, avoiding the spraying vomit. But then it got worse. Large thick streams of yellow ooze flew from his mouth. Sara looked on with her mouth wide open. She waited for Gabe to finish and watched as he walked away, and sat cross-legged on the floor.

"Gabe, are you all right?" She rushed to his side and shook him. "It's the tall man." She looked to either side.

Gabe sat motionless. Though his eyes were open, only the whites were showing—he might as well have been sleeping, or dead. Wherever he was, he was not in the windmill with Sara. Sara shook him, trying to get his attention, but it was useless—like the side of a mountain, he wasn't about to move.

Sara tried to rub the tears from her eyes, but they kept coming, streaming down her cheeks. She sat next to Gabe, shook him by the shoulders, and said, "What have I done? My God, what have I done?"

CHAPTER ELEVEN

When Sara awoke the next morning, birds were singing and the sun shone through the splintered opening of the windmill. She softly rubbed her eyes and looked for Gabe, but he was gone. "Gabe," she called out and walked around the windmill. "Gabe, where are you?" She continued walking.

Gabe was down by the stream kneeling at its edge, and looking at his reflection wavering in the shimmering water. He felt closer to nature than ever before, as if he were waiting for this all his life. He also felt a deep peacefulness within himself, which he had never felt before.

"Maybe this is what it feels like to be reborn," he said and continued to look at his reflection.

He thought back to the scene at the windmill with the sound of the baby, but then the reflection staring back at him changed to that of Sara's. Gabe shook his head and closed his eyes for a few seconds, but when he opened them, Sara's face still stared back at him. Hearing someone coming, Gabe stood and looked over his shoulder.

"Sara, is that you?" he called out and stumbled over rocks and rough dirt as he made his way up the steep hill. He slipped, regained his balance, stumbled, and made it to the top of the hill.

As if he hadn't seen her in weeks, his heart raced, and his

breath grew shorter. He stood with the sun beating down on his back and neck. A cool breeze blew in his face. Birds sang. Gabe inhaled and smiled. "Sara!" he said, still trying to catch his breath. "You'll never guess what just happened to me!" He slurred his words, making it hard for her to understand him.

"Now take it easy, Gabe, and tell me what happened."

He turned around and pointed at the water below them. "I was just looking at the peaceful water, and I saw your face shimmering in it." Gabe shook his head and gasped. "Am I going crazy?"

Her eyebrows rose. "If you're going crazy, then I'm already crazy."

"What happened to me in the windmill last night?" Gabe stared intently at her.

Sara looked down. "I'm not sure. But I know it has to do with the tall man. Remember that sickening smell in the windmill?" Sara said and shivered.

Gabe's nose twitched. "Of course I do. It's not something you'd soon forget—though I'd like to."

"That smell could have meant only one thing."

"And what's that?"

"It's the tall man's rotted soul escaping. He's the evil that walks. Lately I've been dreaming about him. He's the man we spoke with last night. The man you talked with. He's been stalking me at the museum too."

"I know I've seen him there too. Sara, I want to know who he is and why he's after you. I asked him but he wouldn't tell me."

Sara took a deep breath. "His soul is trapped in human form. He was punished a very long time ago and damned to walk the earth for eternity. That was before he sold his soul to the devil. He made a deal to stop people like me, and in return he would get his freedom back."

"This is incredible, Sara. Would you happen to know what he did to become damned?"

"He was one of the men who tortured Christ. His damnation was his punishment."

"You know, come to think of it, he did mention your history was as old as the Crucifixion." Gabe paused and looked at her. "Did you know him way back then?"

Sara shook her head. "I believe so. But when you have as many images in your waking and sleeping hours as I do, you tend to lose track of what you were. The angel I spoke with the other night told me if I did remember everything I've been through, it would kill me. She only came to me in an attempt to stop me from losing my mind altogether."

Sara stared, walked up to him, and touched his hair.

"What are you doing?" Gabe said and pulled away.

"Your hair. It's gray," she said and looked on. "Come over here, out of the light." She motioned him over.

Gabe followed her to a shaded area a lofty pine tree provided. Sara looked closer and saw even more this time. "I thought so," she said and walked around him. "My God," escaped her lips. "Look at your feet," she said and brought her hands up to cover her mouth.

Gabe's feet were bruised on the top and bleeding, and his toenails were filled with black earth. He raised his eyebrows. "I guess I couldn't find my shoes."

"We've got to get you home. Your feet need to be cleaned before they get infected. My God, Gabe, didn't you feel that?" Her mouth was wide open.

Gabe shook his head and continued to stare down at his feet. *How could this have happened without me knowing about it,* he thought. "Listen, Sara. It doesn't matter. Other than my art, and my mother, you're the only thing I really care about. I'll go with you across the country and to the stars."

Sara smiled and said, "Before we do anything, we must get home. Your feet need to be cleaned and bandaged, or you won't be in any shape to travel across the street no less to the stars with me. Now, come on. Let's go."

"You're going to have to help me, Sara. My feet all of a sudden are burning like fire. But why didn't I notice this before?"

Sara shook her head.

###

Together they walked along the edge of the water and through the dirt path that led back to Sara's house. "What was that?" Sara asked, and they both stopped.

"Sounded like a branch cracking," Gabe said and looked.

All he saw were a few birds snipping at bugs on the ground, and a squirrel that scurried up the nearest tree.

"It's the tall man," Sara said. "Stay here." She headed back up the trail and disappeared in the thick brush.

Gabe waited, and a few minutes later he heard footsteps and looked up.

"Where did you go?" Gabe asked, staring at her.

"I went looking for him, but I didn't see him. But I did find large footprints in the mud."

Gabe looked over his shoulder. "We have to get away from him."

"It's not that easy. It's not as if you can just move to the next town. Wherever I go he will follow." Sara shook her head. "Let's get you home," she said, and glared at where she had come from.

###

A few minutes later, Sara and Gabe came out on the other side of the woods, which led directly into Sara's back yard. A thin mist hovered a few inches off the grass. Sara looked back toward the woods from which they had just emerged.

Gabe felt exhausted by the time they reached the edge of Sara's lawn. He took a deep breath and nearly fell from her arms, which had to be numb and powerless from the trip. After a brief rest, they walked the rest of the way to the back of Sara's house.

"You stay here," she said, and walked into the house.

Gabe sat there when all of a sudden he started shaking. "What is that stink?" he said and rubbed his nose. "My God," he said and reached for his stomach, which felt like it had just dropped. "Wow," he said and was lifted in the air and flown through the backyard like a bird.

In seconds, he was back at the edge of the grass by the woods. "Ouch," he expelled as he tried to walk. "What the hell is going on?"

Gabe looked at the woods and thought he saw something move. He squinted but all he saw and heard were leaves crackling.

"Gabe," he heard Sara call out a minute later. "Gabe, where are you?"

"Sara, I'm over here at the edge of your yard by the woods," he said and waved.

Gabe saw Sara running toward him, and waved some more. When she got there, she stood with her hands on her hips, and inhaled deeply.

"Why did you leave, Gabe?" Sara took another breath and shook her head.

"I didn't. I was flown to this spot by what, I don't know," Gabe said and wiped the sweat from his forehead.

"Say, what? . . ."

"Sara, what's going on here?"

"I—"

There was a flash of bright light, and Sara pushed Gabe out of the way. She was engulfed in a lightning bolt that slammed her to the ground. The resulting exploding sound deafened Gabe. With his ears covered, he looked over at Sara where she lay still. Her clothes were charred and smoldering, and her chest was scorched where she had been hit. Gabe looked at the woods, but all he saw was a flash of dark clothing go by.

Sara's father burst out of the house, dressed in a bathrobe and slippers, and ran over to the two. He looked at Gabe and then at his daughter. "What happened?" he asked and knelt at Sara's side.

"You'll never believe this, but a bolt of lightning struck your daughter." Gabe said, still in shock himself.

Sara's father looked up at him, toward the sky, and then to his daughter. Johnny slumped over her body and started to cry.

Gabe saw her eyes start to slowly flutter like butterflies. Gabe looked hard, feeling it was his mind playing tricks, but after a few seconds he realized this was really happening. Then the wound to her chest started to make a gurgling, sucking sound. This drew the attention of both Gabe and Johnny. He slowly let go of his daughter and pulled away even slower. He was still on his knees as he looked down at Sara and then at the shrinking wound to her chest.

Sara's eyes opened. Somehow life was slowly breathed back into her. The wound to her chest was now healing at an impossible rate. In a minute, the wound was completely healed. Only a small scar remained. The only things to indicate that Sara had been hit were the blood on her clothes, and the burns to her shirt.

She looked at both her father and then Gabe, who both looked as white as fallen snow. She slowly sat up, still not saying a word. She looked around and then felt the area of her chest. She unbuttoned her shirt a little to see, but there was nothing but a blemish there now. "I really don't know where to start," she said, looking mostly at her father. "Dad, you thought I was crazy, but after I tell you what I'm about to, I think you're going to change your mind," Sara said and tried to crack a smile. "Remember when mother and Susan died?" Her father nodded. "Do you also remember that I was in the car with them?" Her father nodded a second time. "Well, I died in that car too." She paused. "No! Sara died in that car."

"What do you mean Sara died in that car? You are Sara, aren't you? Standing right before me!" Johnny had a puzzled look on his face, like a child at school who doesn't understand what the teacher has just said.

"Does that mean you're an angel?" Gabe asked with a hint of excitement present in his voice.

Sara smiled and said, "I guess you could call me that, but I'm different things to different people. I could be a lover to some," she said and looked hard at Gabe, "a daughter yet to others," she said and looked at Johnny.

"So you're not my Sara," Johnny said and looked at her hard.

"No, no, no," Sara said, stood, and brushed off her pants. "I'm everything she ever was. Believe me, what I experienced happens to many people. In fact, it happens all the time. We're just not aware of it when it does," she said, doing her best to explain it so they would understand.

"If so, then why are you aware of it?" her father asked.

"That's a good question," she said. The wind blew her hair into her face. "Why do some people excel at one thing and others do not? Why do siblings raised in the same household have different abilities?" Sara said and pushed her hair out of her face.

"Sara, I hear what you're saying, but it's hard to swallow. I'm your father," he said, and paused. "You are my daughter!" He continued to stare.

"Listen," Sara said and slammed her hands at her sides. "I think all of this has you confused. Everything about me, including my memories, is Sara, except my soul. When she died in that car wreck, my soul entered her body. So the sooner you get this through your head, the sooner you will understand me."

"I still don't get it," Gabe said and looked back and forth between Sara and her father. "Who gets to pick which person is going to be saved? People die all the time, and all they do is wind up seven feet under. What about them?"

"What you ask is yet another good question, but it's a question I don't have the answer to. Why does the sun rise every day? Why do people kill each other? Why do babies starve? Things happen for a reason. That I know is true. For the longest time, I felt I was just going crazy. Now I finally understand that I wasn't." She smiled.

Gabe watched as Sara's father stood there, studying her.

But no matter how much he looked at her, it was Sara. She had a light brown birthmark on her right forearm, just above the crook where the arm bends—that was there. When she was seven years old, her mother had let her stir hot pudding on the stove. Somehow Sara managed to spill it all over her left hand—scalding it bad. The scars from that day never went away, and they too were exactly where they belonged.

"Then could you please tell me why you jumped into Sara's body?" Gabe asked.

She took a deep breath. "I already told you, I don't know, but I know it was for a reason."

"Now I understand why you're so frustrated. This is the most incredible thing I've ever seen, and if I hadn't seen it with my own eyes, I wouldn't believe it was true."

"But knowing what we now know, what are we supposed to do?" Johnny asked.

"Nothing."

Johnny sighed. "You've got to be kidding. Maybe it's easy for you, but how can I possibly live my life the way I did before I found out all of this?" He pointed a finger at her.

Sara moved closer to her father and said, "I'm sorry, but there isn't a thing I can do about what you saw." She started to move away, but Gabe grabbed her.

"Where are you going?" he said.

She paused as she looked over her shoulder with a smile and said, "I'm going home to get something to eat and then some sleep. Even I need sleep, and then I'm going to see Winnie at the hospital. You're free to join me if you like." Sara turned and walked back to the house.

CHAPTER TWELVE

After Gabe got home and lied to his mother about where he had been all night, he tended to his feet, had a quick bite to eat, and went straight to bed.

###

Gabe's heavy eyes opened to a darkened room. When he leaned over to see the clock, he snapped up, thinking it was still morning. He quickly got up to open the blinds to let the sun fill his room, but when he opened them, he realized the sun was on the other side of the house.

"I can't believe how late it is," he said standing in front of the window. He stretched and yawned, rubbing the sleep from his eyes, then put on a pair of sweats and a ragged tee shirt.

"How many times do I have to tell you, you sleep too late. You had a phone call a few hours ago, but when I tried to wake you, you refused to get up. So I took this message down for you," his mother said, and handed him a piece of paper. Gabe took the paper from her hands and opened his eyes wide to see his mother's shaky writing.

"I can't believe an art agent saw my paintings at the library. I didn't think anyone went into that room." Gabe was so happy that he kissed his mother on the cheek and pulled away, smiling.

"Oh, and by the way, Sara called twice. She seemed a bit upset that you were still sleeping. I told her that as soon as you got up, I'd let you know that she called. But I must warn you again. You'd better stay away from girls. Now go and call her so you don't make me out to be a liar."

Sometimes you can be as mixed-up as the weather, Gabe thought.

"How's Sara's grandmother making out?"

This was about all the shock that Gabe could handle for one day. "I really don't know, though the last time I saw her, she looked pretty good. She's a sweet old lady. I hope she's okay. Let me give Sara a call," he said and disappeared into the kitchen and dialed her number.

"Hello," Sara's voice said.

"Sara, it's me, Gabe. I'm sorry I didn't call sooner, but I've been sound asleep since I last saw you. I haven't slept that much in years."

"I know what you mean. How's everything?"

"Well, as they say, it's been an education. How is your father taking it?"

"He's been kind of quiet since yesterday morning. I guess I can't blame him. I just hope he snaps out of it. You know, since the other night at the windmill I've been having visions—you'd be surprised at how many families I've been with."

Gabe sat down. "I was wondering about that," he said and looked out the window at a sky that was turning darker by the minute.

"I now understand them as assignments. Some last a few weeks, but most last months, and many times, years. Most times, I never know when it's going to happen. I wish it wasn't like this for me. I'd like to live my life like everyone else does, but I guess that's the price I must pay for immortality."

Gabe could sense the sadness in her words. "I wish I were like you. There are so many things I'd love to do, but I'd need several lifetimes to do them. But if I were like you, I'd have the time—so you've got to tell me how I can be like you. Please, Sara."

She laughed. "What do you think, this is a vacation? What I do is hard work, and believe me, you already have enough to do right now. Some people die before their time. I guess that's where people like myself come in, and in time, where you would have come in. But I can't put that burden on you. I just can't do it."

"So that's what the tall man was talking about. I don't care anymore, Sara. All I want is to be with you."

"I can't do it. It's not my calling, Gabe."

"What happens if I decide to ask for the tall man's help?"

"You would not be welcome into the light."

"The light, what do you mean?"

"Eventually, even people like me have to hang 'em up; if you have done well, you go on into the light, but if you haven't, if you've done bad with your time like the tall man and others like him, then forever will evil and darkness consume you. There is no middle ground here."

The line went silent, and Gabe swallowed hard. "Are you talking about heaven and hell?"

"I guess you could call it that, but I have much simpler words for it—lightness and darkness. I love you with all my heart, but we can never be together like you want us to."

"I want to be with you, Sara, but I didn't know it was going to be so difficult. Isn't there another way?"

"None that I know of."

"Couldn't you transform and be like me?"

"I don't know if that's possible, but even if it was, I've made a commitment to what I am and what I've got to do. When the time is right, I'll know it."

Her answer wasn't what Gabe was looking to hear. Here he was willing to risk his own existence. He sighed and shook his head. "Couldn't you just abandon your cause and then we could be together."

"That can never be, Gabe. I would be like the tall man if I put my own desires ahead of what I now know I have to do. When it's time for me to move on, I go. Even I grow tired of that way of life. There have been many times when I've wanted to settle down in one place—live my life, grow old, and die like the rest of the world. But I now know that can never be."

The more Gabe thought about Sara's situation, the more he realized why she felt the way she did. "But you're immortal. Do you know what people would do to have that?"

"Everybody wants what they don't have. Immortality is just that. Living like I do, you can never plan on anything. Do you know how many times I've wanted to stay where I was? Not to mention the times when I've fallen in love and not wanted to go away. It's the most frustrating thing to live your life like that."

Gabe could hear Sara's voice growing sadder with each word. "Sara, you are in love with me?"

The line went silent like an old battlefield. The tears Gabe was hearing confirmed what he felt in his heart. She didn't need to say another word. In that instant, Gabe understood why she felt the way she did about her special gift.

"Sara, surely there has to be a way to have the best of both worlds. Haven't you ever talked to anyone who might know of a safe way to do this?"

"A safe way! You act if we're crossing a traffic-jammed street. This is life and death here," Sara said and sniffled.

"How do you know when you're in contact with someone such as yourself?"

"It starts with a feeling I get inside. It's like a warm sensation in your stomach, but sometimes it's different."

"When was the last time you took over someone's body before the one you now occupy?"

"From what I remember it happened last with the Johnsons, in upstate New York. Their son fell down a well. He should have died, but instead I came out in his body. They were all amazed and talked about it for weeks and months after it happened. They called me God's gift. It was a special time with that family. From what I understand, his first son went on, years later, to invent a farm machine that they still use today. This is the good part of what I like to call the 'trapping.'"

"You sure picked the right word for it. Now I understand why what you do is so important. And I understand why you cannot interfere with my life. Saving people is much more important than our love for each other.

"I know, Gabe. You don't know how much I feel at peace now that I fully understand what I am. I just wish I could have found out sooner. You know how everything has two sides to it. You know, like good and evil, positive and negative."

"Yes," Gabe agreed.

"Well, there are people just like me running around causing havoc, death, and destruction as well—people like the tall man. It's a battle I hope will never end."

"How could you say such a thing," Gabe snapped and got up.

"You've got me all wrong. I was just trying to say that good and bad forces are constantly pulling at each other like magnetic fields, but if one of them becomes stronger than the other, you have an imbalance. Look back in time and you can see when this has happened. When there's a great imbalance between the two, conflict and war break out. The only problem we have today is that we never know when the good is mounting. You don't read it in the papers, and you hardly ever see it on the television or in movies. It's sad, but it's the truth."

Gabe shook his head. "You sure said a mouthful."

"Listen, I'm going over to see Winnie at the hospital. I should be back around three thirty. I'd like to see you then if that's okay with you. This way you have some time to think about what we just discussed."

"Sure, I'd love to see you later this afternoon, but I've got a call to make. There's an art agent who's interested in my paintings. He saw them at the Southwick Library. Six months ago, I won a contest for a couple of my paintings. Part of the prize was displaying my work at the library. It may be nothing, but you never know. I'll call you to let you know what I'm doing. If I don't have the time this afternoon, I'd love to see you tonight. Say hello to Winnie for me, will you."

"You bet I will, and good luck with the agent."

Gabe hung up the phone, got showered and dressed, and made

the call. The agent set up a meeting at the museum and arranged to use a viewing room for it. He told Gabe to bring what he thought was his best work.

Gabe put together some sketches, a few small paintings, and slides of his best larger paintings. He felt important like never before. He dressed in blue slacks, and a white shirt and matching tie. Though his neck felt tight, he still felt good. A little nervous, but good.

###

Gabe pulled into the museum and killed the engine. He wiped his brow as he crossed the parking lot and confidently strode up the front steps with a slight limp, holding his black leather portfolio.

"Gabe Chaplin," a thin voice said from the top of the steps.

Gabe looked up to see a short man standing. *This must be John Wilson*, he thought. He looked nothing like what Gabe had envisioned. He was an older man, in his fifties, with short gray hair and small brown eyes. But something was familiar about him.

"John Wilson," Gabe said, and looked at him.

"That's me. Nice to meet you, Gabe." He extended a hand and Gabe shook it.

"Why don't we go inside and take a look at your work. I'm excited about seeing what you've brought. If it's anything like what I saw at the library, you're going to have one hell of a career as an artist," he said and smiled.

Inside, the museum was as still as a forest. Gabe followed John toward the main desk. The place still smelled new like a car off the lot. The black-and-white tile floor was so shiny it looked wet. It also reflected the light coming in from the skylights above. The flying buttresses overhead were high as mountaintops, and the Doric columns standing tall and proud looked as if they really had been made thousands of years before.

They stopped at the main desk. "My name is John Wilson. I called earlier about using a room in your study. If I remember correctly, we will be using it for half an hour," he said and smiled.

The girl snapped her gum and cocked her head. "Are you sure we haven't met before?" she asked in a thin nasal voice.

He raised his eyebrows and smiled. "Maybe you saw me walking around the museum. I sure have been around here enough."

She snapped a bubble and consulted her computer screen. "It says you've rented room 306 for half an hour. The room is just around the corner and down the stairs, you'll see a big red door," she leaned over the counter and pointed. "Go through that door and through the next. In that room will be a series of doors on either side. Room 306 will be the third on your left," she said and sat back down. "It also says that the rest of the balance, which is forty-five dollars and fifty nine cents, is now due—plus admission."

John shook his head. "You sure have one heck of a racket here, don't you?" John pulled out a slim black leather wallet, from which he removed a credit card. "You take MasterCard, I hope."

She took the card off the counter and swiped it. "Of course. Is he also with you?" she asked, nodding at Gabe.

John nodded, and she handed him the key.

A white slip was provided, and John quickly signed it. She returned his card, along with a receipt, and said, "Have a nice day."

"I hope you're good with directions because I haven't a clue as to where I'm going. I'd get lost in a one-road town," John said and laughed.

Gabe took the lead. "I can at least get us to that red door she spoke of, though I've never been in the viewing rooms before. So, what brings you to the little old town of Southwick? You seem like a fish out of water."

"Really? Some of the greatest creative minds came from small towns just like Southwick. I'm what you might call a scout. Didn't you apply to some big art schools in New York?"

"I applied to the School of Visual Arts and NYU in New York City. I was accepted to both but had to stay here for personal reasons, though I'm doing fine with the local college. But I'd have to say that I learn more on my own at this point. They're just not up to my speed anymore."

They descended the stairs and headed for the red doors.

All at once, hordes of people were everywhere. It was so tight that they had to turn to their sides to squeeze by. Once inside with the lights on, room 306 was spacious. It had three chairs in it, a computer, a shelflike desk that was screwed into the wall, and to the right of the computer was a small silver light box for slides and transparencies. The wall provided several outlets mounted just above the desk, and a posted notice stating that computer printouts could be collected at the main desk for a charge of $2.50 each. The walls were painted in an off-white with a gray carpet that was thick and stain resistant. There were adjustable dome lights high above.

"Not bad!" John said and took out a small black plastic case he had in the pocket of his suit jacket.

Inside the case were a couple of floppy disks. He opened it, placed it on the desk, and turned on the computer. He waited for it to boot up and inserted a disk.

"You can take out your work while I bring this up on the screen. It's just administration stuff. I hope you don't mind answering some boring but necessary questions?"

"No, not at all," Gabe said and proceeded to take out his slides and place them on the light box. He flipped the red switch on the side, and there was his art on display. Gabe answered a few questions and couldn't wait to get started. His stomach twitched with excitement.

"Now let's see what we have here," John said and slid his chair over and gazed. "How long have you been painting?"

"Let's see, I'd say since the first grade. You'd have to ask my mother for anything before that." Gabe smiled.

"So you've been painting for at least fifteen years then, right?" John still couldn't take his eye off Gabe's work.

Gabe shook his head. "I guess you could say that."

"You're quite talented. This is some of the best work I've seen in years, and I've seen art from all over the world. Some day your work will be in a museum, just like this one," he said and touched a finger to the table. Gabe raised his eyebrows. At this point in life, all he wanted to do was earn a living with his art. A lot of poor artists wound up in museums.

"Your paintings have a dreamlike quality to them. Are they dream inspired?" John asked, still looking.

"You know, some of them are. Like this one for instance," Gabe said and pointed to the second row, third from the left—which was a painting of a man dressed in a space suit floating around in space. The painting was large at one by two feet. The figure looked so real it seemed like it would jump off the slide.

"You had a dream of floating around in space—is that how it went?"

"Kind of. I always dream about space and floating around weightless. Maybe I should have been an astronaut," Gabe joked.

"If you sat there and told me you've been painting for a lifetime, I'd believe you. This is extraordinary work for a man of any age, no less yours." Gabe felt like a million bucks.

"Listen, Gabe. The way I see it, you'll draw the interest of many galleries in New York City. That's the best way to go at this point. Let them hash it out. Then we come in and take the highest bidder. We'll play them against each other. This way, we'll get more up front." The more Gabe listened to John, the more he felt like he was a used-car salesman, but there was definitely something else about John, something Gabe couldn't put his finger on.

"You can make a ton of money here and say good-bye to this shit-kicking town forever. Isn't that what you want?"

Gabe looked right through him. He took it in stride, but his silence let John know he didn't appreciate what he had just said about his town. It was like when someone said a bad thing about the place you grew up in. You knew it was bad, but you didn't like anyone saying it, especially an outsider.

"Listen," Gabe said and sat up. "I think this is moving way too fast for me. I don't think I'm ready for the big-time art world just yet. I've got a lot on my mind, and I still have school to finish up with. I don't care how much money you have for me—I'm finishing up with school and then I'll pursue my art career at my own speed."

"Whoa, whoa, just wait a minute here," John said and jumped

out of his seat. "I'm not asking you to quit school in the least. We can get the ball rolling while you finish school. That's not a problem at all," he said. The veins in his forehead bulged with every word he spoke.

Gabe had to admit, if he could stay in school and pursue the galleries of New York City, that would be fine by him. He did need the money, and just maybe he could go to the art school he always wanted to.

"Just think it over, Gabe. This is the chance of a lifetime. And believe me, I've seen them come and go." His brown eyes stared. "You've got to take advantage of what comes your way. Just remember, what's here today might be gone tomorrow," John said and pointed a finger at him.

"Okay I'll think this over, but if I did agree, what about my work? How will it get to New York? And who's going to pay for it?"

John smiled and said, "Don't worry about a thing. We'll ship it next-day air. If you like, you'll only have to come down on opening night. I'll even arrange for your family to come too." When he smiled his face creased with deep valleys and craters like those of the moon. "I'll also pick up the tab and bill you later when the sales of your work start to come in," John turned off the computer, grabbed his disk, and got up. "You think about it, but like I said, don't let the chance of a lifetime pass you by."

"I'll definitely think about it." Gabe gathered his work, turned, and opened the door.

Gabe's eyes widened, and Sara stepped back and stared at John.

"What are you doing here, Sara?" Gabe's smile grew larger by the second.

"Shouldn't I be asking you that?"

Gabe turned toward John and introduced the two. Sara shook his hand and her body swayed slowly like a tree in the wind. But still Sara was cool as a breeze on a hot summer day.

"I'll be staying in town for another couple of days. Here's my number." John scribbled it down on a piece of paper and handed it to Gabe. "So do give me a call as soon as you can to let me know what you're going to do. It was nice meeting with you," John shook Gabe's hand, glared at Sara, and walked away.

Sara smiled, but her smile was one of those put-on ones kids tend to do when they're forced to.

The museum was now busy, so Gabe and Sara had to just about yell at each other in order to be heard. "Could we go outside and talk? My bike broke, so I have a cab waiting out front. Can you take me home?"

"Of course," Gabe said and zipped up his portfolio.

They walked through the crowded museum and out the front door. "There it is," Sara said and pointed to the yellow cab. "He's been waiting there since I got here ten minutes ago. I only have twelve dollars and some loose change in my pockets," Sara said and started to take out her money. "I'm sure that, with all this waiting, the fare is going to be more than that."

"Pay him with what you have, and if you need any more, I'll pay the rest."

"Thanks," she said and smiled.

It was a little after midday, and the sun was high in a cloudless sky that was a rich wall of fading cerulean blue to a pink-orange. The colors looked intense like a matte painting for a major motion picture.

Gabe and Sara walked over to the cab and saw the cabby's arm hanging out the window. A newspaper was folded over his stomach, and the radio played in the background in a wall of hissing static. Gabe poked the cabby in his fleshy arm, causing him to wake with a jolt. He knocked over the newspaper, and looked to his left with blinking eyes.

"What? What?" He sat up and wiped his eyes.

"Here's my fare," Sara said, handing the money to him.

The cabby grabbed it from her, counted it, then looked at the meter. "You're five dollars and thirty-five cents short. And I don't take no credit cards," he added and reached on the seat next to him for a pack of cigarettes.

"Here you go, Sara," Gabe said and reached into his pocket. "You owe me lunch," he told Sara with a smile and handed the cabby his money.

"What about a tip? I've been waiting out here all day," the man said and blew smoke like a train running through town. Gabe threw him another five dollars and told him to have a nice day. The man smiled, started the taxi, and raced away with a screech. Both of them covered their ears.

"Sara, what's wrong?" Gabe asked, knowing something was out of synch by the blank stare on her face.

Sara took a deep breath and said, "I just don't know." She turned away and walked.

Gabe followed, grabbed her by the arm and said, "Sara, what's going on?" Then he thought, *Her grandmother. Something happened to her grandmother.* "Sara, is Winnie all right?" Gabe now stood in front of her, but Sara looked away, hiding her teary blue eyes.

The sun shone through the leaves, and with a soft breeze, an elaborate design of shadows danced over Sara's face. She wiped her eyes and looked at Gabe. "It's not Winnie at all. In fact, she's doing quite well." She again wiped the tears from her eyes. "It's that man you were just with."

"What do you mean?" Gabe asked and stepped away. "He's just an art agent. I was meeting with him to discuss the selling of my work."

"Is that who you really think he is?"

Gabe shrugged. "Who else am I supposed to think he is. That's how we were introduced," Gabe said and leaned up against a tall maple tree that was covered in a thick black fungus. Gabe didn't want to hear any negatives about the man he just met. He saw meeting him as a way of finally getting out of Southwick on his own terms; he would have no excuse not to, this time. And if he made enough money, even his mother would understand that.

"I'm sorry. I didn't mean to upset you. But I'm only telling you the truth. Whoever he told you he was, it was a lie. He's the tall man," she said and sat down cross-legged.

A gust of wind blew hard, cooling their warm skin. For a moment, neither of them said a word. It was quiet except for the wind shaking leaves above, and a few passing cars. Far off, kids shouted as they played.

Gabe turned, looked at Sara, and said, "If it *is* him, why is he changing his appearance?" Gabe paused and added, "And what does this have to do with me?"

Sara picked at the grass, looked up and said, "I don't know. But I know it has to do with stopping me."

"Why can't he just walk up to you and do whatever it is he wants to?" Gabe let out an exasperated breath.

"We need each other, like night and day. It's just so confusing." Sara shook her head.

"What could you possibly need with a man like that?" Gabe shivered.

"I'm the last of a special race of thirteen angels. For over a thousand years, we have walked the earth. The tall man has destroyed the other twelve. I'm the last one he has to destroy to free his tormented soul. His face may change, but I know it's him underneath. No matter what mask he wears, I can always see his true face," she said and continued to pick at the blades of grass.

Gabe shook his head. "I'm a little lost. Why would he try to kill me?"

"From the other night, he knew I was trying to help you become like me, and he just couldn't let that happen. I can assure you that all he touches is destroyed."

"If this is true, why did you have to get me involved with this? All I ever wanted to do was be a painter," Gabe said and looked away.

"Love! I fell in love with you, Gabe, and I'm tired of leaving things behind." Sara rose and started to walk away. Gabe walked over to her and pulled her close, then kissed her.

Sara smiled. "I never thought in a million years this could happen."

"Is there any way to stop him?"

"Yes, there is one way, but it's very dangerous to those involved."

Gabe gritted his teeth and clenched his fists. "Can you tell me? I'd like to try. I'm already close, and he doesn't know that I'm on to him. Even if he does, it doesn't matter." Gabe stared at her.

Sara shook a finger at him. "Listen to me, Gabe, and listen good. He's going to attempt to take your body, but he's going to need you to give it freely. If not, he could be destroyed in the process. But just remember, the moment he touches you, you must be able to think only pure thoughts—you have to push your will on him. The moment he's out of his old body and entering yours is when he will be at his weakest. You will only have a few seconds to force him out. At that point, he will have nowhere to go and be trapped as if floating in space. Remember, Gabe, your mind has to be totally focused on what I just told you. No other thoughts. Now, are you sure you can do this?"

"I'm sure I can, Sara. Anything to be with you," he said and kissed her.

CHAPTER THIRTEEN

One day had passed since Gabe met John Wilson at the museum. At Gabe's request, they met for something to eat at Joan's Diner. Families sat in tight booths eating stacks of pancakes and waffles, with melted squares of butter and blueberry preserves thickly spread, side orders of crispy golden home fries, and thin greasy wet sausages. Truckers in blue jeans and thick wool shirts sat on fixed stools along the bar near the entrance. Smoke curled above them in plumes, mixing with the aromas of hamburgers, steak, and home fries.

Gabe and John sat by a window and waited to be served. The view was the south side of Route 58, where all the eighteen-wheelers were parked in rows as far as the eye could see. "Do you eat here regularly?" John asked, looking over the place.

"Whenever I get someone to pay for it." Gabe laughed.

A waitress with dark eyes set in deep sockets walked up to their table. "What will it be, fellas?" she said, looking John over. He was an outsider, and it looked like the waitress knew it.

"I guess I'll have a cup of coffee," John said and turned to Gabe.

"That's all you're ordering? They have the best homemade apple pie in town. You've got to try it," Gabe insisted.

John shook his head. "Okay I'll have a slice of apple pie too." The waitress took their orders and left.

"Listen, I've got a question for you. Which agency do you work for? Before I get involved, I want to know whom you work for, and I'd like to speak to some of your clients—just to get a feel for what you and your agency can do for me." Gabe might as well have asked John to swallow a full ear of corn sideways.

John cleared his throat and shifted in his seat. "I work for myself. It keeps the costs down." Gabe shook his head. "Okay, to tell you the truth, I don't have many clients. In fact, at the moment, I don't have any at all."

"I could have told you that much. If you don't tell me why you're really here, I'm walking out that door," Gabe said and rose.

John extended his arm and said, "There's no need for that. Now, just sit down and I'll tell you everything."

Gabe stood there for a moment, just to make him wait. He calmly sat down and said, "Why should I believe anything you say. You've already given me a song and dance. And if I hadn't caught on, I would have fallen for it—hook, line, and sinker."

"I just don't . . . know where to start."

"How about with the truth. That's always a good place." Gabe eyed him hard.

John's eyes were blood-shot, yellow, and cloudy. His face was puffy and creased, and there were dark brown stains under his eyes. "How old do you think I am?" John asked abruptly.

Gabe cocked his head. "I guess I'd have to say mid-fifties. Yeah, mid-fifties."

"That's not a bad guess. But I've asked you a trick question—would you care to try again?" John said with a cocky smile.

"Listen, obviously we're not on the same page. So why don't you just spit it out. I don't like riddles," Gabe said angrily.

John sat back in a huff, and shook his head. "I'm much older than I could ever look. Not only that, but I'm older than all the people in this diner put together," John said and looked all around.

Before John could elaborate, the waitress came back with their orders. She placed them on the table and left.

"I don't know how to tell you this, but I've been chasing people through time. I capture their dark spirits and put an end to their destruction. That's my job," John said and sipped his coffee and ate a slice of apple pie. "Not bad," he said in between bites. He licked his lips.

"See, I told you the apple pie was good." Gabe took a bite of his own. "Now, that's one hell of a story you just told," he said and almost choked on a mouthful of pie. Gabe cleared his throat and sipped some ice water and continued, "So I guess you're here for Sara."

"What are you talking about?" John said with a shake of his head and a smile.

"Listen, don't play games with me. I know that you tried to kill me a few days ago, and I know you're not an art agent, so don't bother to deny that either. I know who you are," Gabe said with the power and vigor of a president conducting a speech. He sliced a hefty piece of pie and slowly chewed it, savoring every taste as if it were the last piece on earth. He let out a deep breath and smiled.

"So you know the truth. I have to look at the big picture. Millions of lives hang in the balance. I guess you're not aware of what's going on here. Then again, how could I expect you to understand," John said in displeasure.

"I'm confused about one thing. Who chose for you to become what you are?"

John's gray bushy eyebrows rose. "That's a very good question." He smiled. "It's not like someone comes up and tells you, 'Here you go, kid. For the next couple of thousand years, you're going to hunt down such and such people. Good luck.' It's nothing like that at all. It's like having another sense. The moment you become aware of it, you keep questioning it, until you find there are others like you. I've met my share through time. You know, I was one of the first people to work on nuclear development long before people knew what it was. I remember the day I jumped into Dr. Smith's body as if it were only yesterday. He should have died in an experiment. You should have seen the looks on their faces when I walked out of that explosion. Before that day, I'd had some interesting experiences, but this one was the best of all. From that day on, I hoped it would never end. Anyway, when I jumped into this body," he said pointing to himself, "I had no idea who or what I was saving. I was just eager to do what I was doing. This assignment was different from all the rest." His look became hard. Reflecting on his past, he appeared to look younger.

Gabe could see the sadness pouring out of this man as he spoke about his past and seemingly nearing end.

"I had to keep reminding myself how good this last assignment was and that helped me along. Nobody knows this, but in the late eighties, we were minutes away from nuclear war with the USSR, when it was still called that. The powers that be wanted the cold war to go one forever but realized Russia could no longer afford Communism. War is about money and power. Russia had the power but lacked the money to support it. Less than a year later, the Berlin wall fell. Nuclear war with Russia was no longer an option. That decision put many people out of a job, but I managed to stay put. There were some who still felt that nuclear war with Russia could be carried out, and, might I add, there are some even today who still think like that. What do you think all that shit in the Gulf was about? Money and power. Nothing more. Nothing less."

Gabe shook his head. *Boy, have I had my head in the clouds?*

"I was one of those hardliners, and I was quite big in my time. You might not believe it, but I had the last say in many war-related situations."

"I thought the president has the last say." Gabe ate a mouthful of pie and washed it down with a sip of water.

John started to laugh from the bottom of his stomach to the ends of the hairs on the top of his head. It took him a full ten seconds to calm down. Even the people across the way looked over. "Where did you ever come up with such an idea? Surely you don't believe that." John said, still trying to check his laughter.

"Listen, I was never one for world politics. Now, what are you planning to do with Sara?

John leaned over the table, his eyes again full of life, "Get one thing through your head—Sara is anything but what she appears to be. Why do you think I've been chasing after people like her for a lifetime trying to destroy them? She's as evil as the devil." John sat back in his seat. "I still can't believe how many bodies she's been through."

Gabe sat up. "What do you mean? She entered those bodies to save people's lives. Sara wouldn't hurt a soul."

John shook his head and laughed under his breath. "She sure has you fooled." He sipped some water.

Gabe sat there, still as the chair he was sitting on. There was just no way he could believe that Sara was anything but good. But if he wanted this game to play on, he had to pretend. He also had to be careful not to seem too drawn in, either.

"Where do I stand in all of this? Surely, a man as capable as yourself doesn't need Gabe Chaplin from the little town of Southwick. I'm still not sure what I can do for you, or why I should even consider doing whatever it is you want me to!"

His eyes bulged. "There's no way I can get closer to her, especially now. But through you I could get as close to her as I need to."

The words "through you" sent a chill through Gabe so that the hairs on the back of his neck stood tall like wild grass. He quickly took a deep breath, swallowed, and said, "What do you mean, through me? Are you saying you'd somehow be in my body?"

"Finally, we're both on the same page," John laced his fingers on the tabletop. "There are two ways for me to transform into another person's body; the first way is to do it without their consent, thus killing them in the process. The second, I could share their body with them and leave it unharmed when I'm finished."

Gabe didn't believe that John was telling the truth about giving his body back when he was done with it, or about what he was saying. He just hoped that he would be able to force him out the way Sara had told him he'd have to.

"What's wrong, kid? Don't you believe me? I see she's got you wrapped around her finger. Like I already told you, don't believe her for a second." John sat motionless as if waiting for Gabe to say the next word.

"I'll think about what you ask, but first you have to do something for me," Gabe said and leaned closer to him. "I wish to be like Sara. I told her about it, and she said she couldn't make that happen."

John smiled and unfolded his hands. "I can help you with your desire," he said, his eyes sparkling. "If you do as I asked, I'll grant your wish."

"Are you sure you're capable of doing that? I know what I ask is out of the ordinary."

John cocked his head back. "You aren't the first. All I want to do is use your body for a few hours and then give it back. Isn't that a small price to pay for the service you'd be doing for your fellow man by ridding the world of people like Sara? And when I'm done, I'll give you what you want." John opened his mouth wide and showed his crooked yellow stained teeth as an animal would before the kill.

Gabe trembled. "Listen, I'd still like to think this over. I want to make sure I'm doing the right thing."

John sat back in his chair and looked like a man who had just been hit below the belt during a prizefight.

"I understand you may need some time to think about this. But when you come back with your answer, it may be too late. This has to be done as soon as possible. For all I know, she may have jumped into someone else's body, and I don't have the time, or the strength, to chase after her anymore. That's why I have to do this now!"

"Listen, let me at least speak to my mother. I want to see her in case something bad happens and I don't have the chance to see her again."

John frowned. "Nothing bad is going to happen to you, Gabe. But if you must see your mother, remember not to take too long. I have a lot of work to do in a short period of time. And don't tell a soul about this," he said, shaking a finger at him. He rose and Gabe followed.

"Where do we meet?"

"I'm staying at the Swanson. I'll be in room 101. You can

come any time you like, but don't take too long. Time is running out!" Gabe quickly scribbled this information down on a napkin, folded it, and put it in his front pants' pocket.

When Gabe left the diner, he felt as if he had done something wrong, and he hadn't done a thing yet. But just being around John was enough to make his skin crawl.

###

Gabe hurried home with a full stomach and a head about ready to explode. His mother met him at the door.

"What's going on, Gabe? One of your professors called today, asking if you were okay. It's not like you to miss class. Something has to be wrong with you. It's that girl, isn't it?" his mother insisted. Gabe shook his head and walked to the kitchen.

"Mother, nothing is wrong with Sara, or at school," he said and opened the refrigerator to get some juice. He took a glass off the counter and sat down. His mother quickly joined him. But before they could talk, Gabe finished his juice and said, "I've got to stop by the art store to pick up some supplies. I'll see you later." He left the house without another word.

What could he really tell her anyway?

###

Gabe got home a half hour later, went straight to his room, and flipped on the radio. He looked over at his painting station, which really was a corner of his room set up with an easel, drawing table and a small desk with supplies, which were always running low. He rolled up his paint tubes like a tube of toothpaste.

Gabe was still shaken from the meeting he had with John. This business about John using his body scared him even worse than those black birds he hated so much. *If John is so powerful, why does he need my body?* This thought played over in Gabe's mind like a hit song, followed by an unexpected one—*Maybe he was telling the truth about Sara.*

CHAPTER FOURTEEN

Sara had called Gabe three times—but since his mother kept saying he wasn't home, she decided to take a ride over, license or no license. Sara's father was at work, doing a double shift, Winnie was still at the hospital, Ralph was sleeping in the den, and Jenna was at a friend's house for the day. So if there was ever a time to drive the car, this was it.

The old Ford pickup was rusted so badly the side panels were threatening to fall off. The windshield had spider cracks on both sides, and the headlights didn't work. For all she knew, it wouldn't even start.

Sara took the keys out of her father's room where he kept them in a cigar box on his desk. Fighting a strong wind, Sara pushed her hair out of her face, got in the pickup, and put the keys in the ignition. She held her breath, turned it, and heard a slight bark. She tried it again and heard an even louder one. She pumped the pedal just like she remembered her father doing and the truck started. It coughed and shook violently, but after a few minutes, it calmed down. Thick clouds of bluish smoke poured out of the rusted exhaust pipes. Sara adjusted the mirrors, looked over her shoulder, and started to back out of the driveway. The truck creaked, shook, and clattered loudly. She drove away with a wall of blue smoke trailing behind. Halfway down the road, she gripped the wheel and did not blink, her eyes wide and staring.

"No, Gabe. You must get away from him. Far away." Her eyes fluttered, and she again saw the road. Swerving out of the way of a lamppost, Sara rode over some high timothy grass, bumped her head on the headliner, and jumped back onto the road with a screech of tires. She looked in the rearview mirror to make sure there were no cars on the road. Fortunately, there weren't. She wiped her sweating brow, took a deep breath, and raced down 58.

###

Gabe was sitting in his bedroom, looking at all the paintings he had done over the years. He had at least twice as many stored downstairs, but there was enough here for him to see what he could lose if things didn't work out with the tall man. Up until he'd met Sara, his painting was all that mattered. That was something he'd thought would never change, but he was still willing to risk it all to spend whatever time he could with her.

Gabe wanted to slip out the back door without his mother seeing. He just didn't want to tell her what he was going to do. He knew that if he tried to lie to her, she'd see through it like tracing paper. On his way out through the kitchen, Gabe looked to his left, then right. But it was too late—Martha was already sitting in the kitchen, sipping a cup of tea and eating crackers.

"Where are you going?" Her eyes locked on him.

Gabe shook his head and took a deep breath. "I'm just going out." He turned away.

"Don't pull that on me. It's that girl, isn't it? How many times have I told you to watch out for girls? I held back some, thinking this one might be different. But they're all the same. She'll just wind up breaking your little heart. You'll see," she said, shaking her head. She sat up, shakily holding her tea. "You'd better tell me where you're going, or I swear I won't let you leave the house." She got up and stood in front of the back door.

Gabe laughed. "Mother, why do you have to do this? I'm going to do whatever I want to, with or without your consent. Now, will you just step aside—I have things to do."

"You're not listening to me. I'm not going to budge until you tell me the truth." She folded her arms.

"I don't know why I'm standing here debating this with you when I can just use the front door," he said and walked toward it.

"No, you can't. It's locked, and I have the key with me," she said, but Gabe had already walked to the front door.

"Mother, I'm not in the mood for any of your games so would you please give me the key to unlock the door. I have something to take care of that I must do on my own."

Martha walked up to Gabe, and he turned around. Her dull eyes fluttered and then stared at Gabe. "Just please tell me where you're going? That's all I ask."

"Listen, I can't get into what I'm about to embark upon," he said and sat down across from her. "You'd think I was nuts—there's just no way you'd believe me. But I can tell you I'm not in trouble with the law, and I'm not running away."

"You must play your mother for a fool. Of course you're not running away! If you were, you'd have your paints in tow, and I don't see any," she said with a sly smile. "Though I can see that whatever it is you're about to do is serious. Just please remember you have a mother here who loves you. That's all I have to say." Martha's smile quickly turned to tears.

Gabe wiped her eyes dry with his hand, and said, "I'll be back, Mother, before you know it." Martha moved out of the way to finally let him by.

###

Ten minutes later, Sara parked in front of Gabe's house and saw that his car was gone. "Maybe his mother knows where he went," she said.

Sara killed the engine and quickly got out of the truck. Outside, a wicked wind blew her hair in all directions. It was as if the wind were trying to stop her from walking. Her hair was in knots by the time she got to the front door. Clouds dark as crow's feathers bloomed across the sky at an alarming speed. Sara looked back at her father's truck and a sky that was now as black as her hair. She banged on the front door, but no one answered. With authority, she banged again and heard some rumbling. The door opened.

"Hello. My name is Sara. I'm the girl who's been calling for the past hour," she said, still fighting the wind. "I'm looking for Gabe. Would you know where he is?" Sara asked and held the hair out of her face so she could see.

"So you're the girl Gabe is always talking about. To tell you the truth, I thought he was with you. Would you care to step in? It's murder out there. Maybe we can figure this thing out together," she said. While Gabe's mother let Sara in, the storm door squeaked and nearly ripped from its rusted hinges.

"I hope wherever Gabe is, he's indoors," his mother said and looked at the angry dark skies. "I've been in this town more years than I care to remember, and I've never heard the wind howl like it now is. This storm sure beats the one back in '59, but I guess you're too young to remember it. I've listened to the weather all day, and not one station said a word about it. But how could they have missed it?" Martha looked away.

"Why don't we go and see what they're saying now," Sara suggested.

She followed Gabe's mother into the living room. Martha flipped on the tube with the clicker and sat back to see the latest report.

"Oh, would you like something to drink?" Martha asked.

Sara waved her hand and said, "No, I'm okay," and sat next to Martha.

There was a special weather report bulletin on the local news station. Gabe's mother quickly found out that only Southwick was experiencing this sudden weather change. Sara shook her head and looked down.

Two seconds later, the screen turned to static snow. Right after that, the power went out, and Martha and Sara found themselves staring at a blank screen. For a long moment, they sat silent.

###

Gabe had just pulled into the parking lot of the Swanson Motel. The sky was dark as if night had fallen upon day. Gabe looked at his watch, but it had stopped. He slowly got out of the car and headed for room 101. The wind was roaring like a thousand angry animals—it seemed to be blowing Gabe in the direction he needed to go. An icy chill ran up his back. With the clouds moving as fast as planes, streaks of bright yellow shone through like giant spotlights, giving off enough light to see every so often—which was all Gabe needed to find room 101.

By the time he got to the door, his heart was thumping, tat, tat, tat, like an overworked piston. Something was telling him to get back in his car, drive away, and never look back, and yet another part of him said to go on and see this through. He swallowed hard, banged on the door, and hoped he was listening to the right voice. All he wanted was to be with Sara without having to look over his shoulder. With John out of the way, this could be a reality. Gabe stood out there in hurricane-like winds but nobody answered. He looked to his left and saw a glowing light. Shadows danced on the drapes in the window. The door opened, and the candle blew out. The scent of burning wax filled the air like perfume.

"I'm glad you could make it, Gabe. I was wondering if you'd ever show up. Why don't you come in," the tall man's voice said from out of the darkness. He searched the top of the dresser for matches and lit the candle.

"You see what's happening outside?" he asked. Gabe looked over his shoulder. *As if I really need to be reminded.*

"I do."

"Do you know what it means?"

Gabe shook his head. "Not really. To me it looks like a pretty bad storm, but it must be something important or you wouldn't be telling me about it, now would you?"

"Have a seat, and I'll let you in on what's happening out there," the tall man said. Gabe sat at the table in front of him.

The room was so dark that Gabe couldn't make out the tall

man's face—all he saw was a black shadow that moved. When he sat down across from Gabe, there still wasn't enough light to see him—but the booming voice was definitely his. Gabe put his hands on the table, and the wind let out an animal-like roar. It was so loud it felt like it was in the room, sitting next to him. For the next thirty seconds or so the hair on Gabe's neck stood at attention. The tall man sat back with his hands behind his head and laughed as if what was happening outside was anything but extraordinary.

"I've never heard wind like that before," Gabe said and looked to either side. "Okay, so what's going on out there?"

The tall man leaned forward and said with deadly calm, "Are you sure you want to know the answer to that question?" He sat back in his seat.

"Is this a game? Of course I do."

"Good," the tall man said and reached for a cigar on the table. "Do you mind if I smoke?" he asked and sparked a match.

"Would it matter if I did?"

Without answering, the tall man inhaled and filled the room with a sweet aroma, and the end of his cigar glowed like the embers of a campfire. In the moment it took him to light up, Gabe did catch a glimpse of what he looked like, and it made his blood run cold and his stomach ache. The skin on his face was gray and falling off, and his eyes were dull like dirty water and sunken in. With every passing second, fear grew in Gabe's heart—a fear the likes of which he had never felt before. His body trembled with it.

"You want to leave, don't you?" a much deeper voice said. He blew cigar smoke in Gabe's face.

Gabe covered his mouth and coughed. "Yes, I'd like to leave. But you're not going to let me, are you?" Gabe said. His hands shook.

"If it's your desire to leave this place, then get up and walk out of here, but if you do, you'll never be able to be like Sara. What I offer is paramount to you, and what I ask in return is a small price to pay. Just think for a moment about what I'm offering. You know, you'll be like a god, Gabe," the tall man said and continued to fill the room with puffy clouds of cigar smoke.

###

"Is everything all right with Gabe? He's been acting pretty strange lately. I always know when there's something wrong with him," Martha said and tapped a finger on the table.

Sara shook her head. "I haven't noticed anything different about him."

"When he left before, he seemed pretty nervous. I thought he might be going to see you, but now that you're here it's got to be something else, but what?"

Martha was rocking back and forth while she sat there talking about Gabe, but she jumped when a branch hit the window. Gabe was her only link to the real world. Without him, she might as well be dead. She really died many years ago after the divorce, which was something she never did recover from—that's why she poured everything she had into Gabe, but it was also why her life had become so empty.

"Would it be okay to take a look in his room? Maybe we'll find something that can lead us to where he might have gone," Sara said. The wind blew, and the house rocked with every breath.

"Sure, let's go. I'm just going to have to make a stop in the linen closet for a flashlight. Could you bring one of those candles too? I'm afraid I'd drop it. My hands are shaking real bad. See?" she said and held them out trembling.

"Are you okay?" Sara asked and reached out to hold Martha still. Martha stood there as if she was in a trance. Her eyes were open and her body still. "Martha, are you okay?"

Martha shook her head. "You'll have to forgive me. My mind plays tricks on me every so often." She began to rub both of her temples in circular motions. "I'll be all right in a minute or so."

"Is there anything I can get you?"

"Well, you could help me over to the kitchen table, and if it wouldn't be too much of a bother, could you get me a glass of water?" Martha's eyes fluttered, and she rubbed her temples again.

Sara helped Martha into the kitchen and walked to the sink.

"Where's the flashlight? I might as well get that too," Sara said and filled a second glass for herself.

"Facing the kitchen sink, it's in the cupboard to your left—though I'm not sure if the batteries still work. If not, you can get the other flashlight in the linen closet in the hallway."

Sara quickly found the flashlight and headed back with it and the two glasses of water. "Here's the water you asked for," Sara said and flipped on the flashlight.

"You know, I don't know what to make of all of this," Martha said and sipped some water. "Do you believe in God?"

Sara leaned forward and sipped her own glass of water. She placed her hands on the table, tilted her head, and said, "God is a relative term, but I'd say I believe in some powerful force that's well beyond our understanding. So if that's what God is to you, then I guess we're on the same page." Sara sipped some more water.

Martha took some time to answer as if an unbelievable weight were on her back. "I don't believe in God like most do, but I do hope someone is looking after my boy." Martha shook her head.

"Why don't we go and check Gabe's room with the flashlight. You might as well lead the way," Sara said and handed it to her. Martha staggered.

"Are you gonna be okay?" Sara reached for her.

She waved her hand. "I'll be fine."

They walked out of the kitchen, down a narrow hallway with two bookcases to their right and a hamper in between, and made a second left into Gabe's room. Sara passed the pictures Gabe had talked about and took a quick glance at them. Martha entered first with the flashlight. She looked inside as if it were for the first time. "'If I'm not home, I don't want you going in my room. Is that understood?' Gabe would always say with a wave of his hand," Martha said, doing her best to imitate Gabe. Sara laughed and looked around Gabe's room too.

"Wow! Did he paint all of these pictures?" Sara asked, her mouth hung open wide like the jaws of a feeding shark.

"He sure did," Martha said and shone the light at a stack of them against the wall. "That's why I know he didn't leave town. He'd never leave all his work behind. Or his paints, for that matter." She looked at them too.

"I had no idea he was that talented," Sara said, still staring.

"How many times do I have to tell him not to throw his dirty clothes on the floor," Martha said and bent with a moan to pick up a pair of white socks, and a pair of washed-out blue jeans. Martha sat on his bed and folded Gabe's pants. The edge of a napkin was sticking out, so she pulled it. Seeing a few letters written in ink, she unfolded it to read the rest. "Here, take a look at this," Martha said and held the napkin out so Sara could see.

"What is it?" Sara asked and walked toward Martha.

"When I went to fold his pants, I found this in his pocket."

Sara took the creased-up napkin from Martha's hand and read what was written on it. "The Swanson, room 101." She looked up. "What would he be doing at such a place?" Sara said and sat next to Gabe's mother. "The Swanson is that run-down motel on 58!"

Sara stared at nothing. "He's there with the tall man!"

"He's there with who?" Martha shook her head.

"I don't have the time to explain."

"Please tell me what's going on with Gabe." Martha breathed heavily, and the veins in her temples pulsed.

Without saying a word, Sara turned and quietly left the room.

Once she opened the front door to leave, a series of powerful winds threatened to pull it from her hand.

"Please tell me what's going on," Martha repeated and walked up behind Sara. Sara looked at the door as it rattled from the wind, and then back at Martha.

"Listen, if it was up to me, I'd tell you, but you wouldn't believe me. Like I already said, I don't have the time either."

Sara could have stayed put if she really wanted to—but Gabe, she had to help Gabe.

She looked at Martha one last time and turned to open the door. Again, it pulled at her hand. "It was nice meeting you, Martha. I hope we have the chance to meet again," Sara said as if she knew that would never happen.

###

"You don't know which way to go, do you? Do what I ask or leave this place."

Gabe swallowed hard. "No, I don't."

"Let me show you something that might help change your mind."

Gabe looked to the wall to his left—projected on it was the front of his house.

"Sara?" Gabe squinted and shook his head. "How did you do that?"

"That's not important, but what Sara will do is," John said.

"What do you mean?" Gabe said.

"Just watch."

Once Sara made it outside, Martha pulled aside the drapes and stuck her face by the window. Sara struggled all the way to the truck. Her hair was all over the place, whipping with the wind. She turned to look one last time and saw Martha staring out the window from the safety of her house, and when their eyes met, Martha opened the drapes all the way and waved.

Sara was struggling to open the door of her truck when she heard a loud crack and saw a tall tree in the front yard come smashing down on the roof of Martha's house. Sara could now see inside, as if it were an egg cracked open. The living room took most of the force. A branch broke off and smashed the front of Martha's television. "No!" Martha screamed.

Gabe stood. "Mother."

The glass tube, which Martha had spent countless hours staring at Oprah Winfrey on, had shattered and lay in hundreds of pieces all over the living room floor. A whirlwind blew inside her house. TV guides, magazines, and paper flew like birds.

Martha raised her hands like Jesus and screamed again. "Not my TV!" A partially broken beam just above her head supported most of the tree's weight, but it gave way with a groan. Martha looked up and screamed, holding her hands up in a vain attempt to stave off her impending doom. The tree hit the floor with a crack, burying her beneath its weight. One arm stuck out from under it, still clutching the remote. Her fingers gradually relaxed, letting it fall to the bloody carpet. A TV guide floated down like a bird and landed on her lifeless body.

Standing at the truck, Sara covered her mouth. She took a step toward the house, but the wind was too strong. "Gabe. You've got to get to Gabe." She struggled to open the door and did after a few tries. She quickly got in and had to work even harder trying to close it. She started the truck and it spit, shook, and threatened to stall like it did before, but she patted the dashboard like you would a pet, and the old clinker stayed running. How far it would go was anyone's guess.

"Mother!" Gabe watched with frozen horror at what had just happened.

"Sara will now come for *you*."

"She wouldn't kill my—"

The tall man stood, his features changed so that he no longer looked anything like he had when Gabe first met him. His face was all bumpy and creased like the bark of a tree, and blood red. The skin on his arms had fallen off—blood dripped out, and muscle and bone peeked through what little skin was left. His once-blue eyes were now dark as the sky outside and as lifeless as the dead. Blood trickled from his puffy red lips. Most of his teeth had fallen out, but the few that hadn't were rotted black, and his gums were swollen and bleeding.

Gabe kept his distance, not wanting a thing to do with what the tall man had become. Then he moved, knocking over the table, and with it, the candle. A low moan started to build into a steady animallike groan. The thing that was once the tall man started to speak. "Don't leave me like this," he said in a voice sounding more artificial than human. Every muscle in Gabe's body tightened like piano strings.

"I guess I've got a lot of explaining to do," the tall man said and moved over to where Gabe stood. Gabe slowly inched his way closer to the door. "I told you, she's not what she pretends to be. She's a fallen angel. That's why she must be stopped. Look at it out there, and it's all because of her."

Gabe took a deep breath and didn't take an eye off of him. "If she's a fallen angel, what are you?"

The tall man laughed a laugh that sounded like popping bubbles. "I am also an angel, a good one. Believe me, she'll do more than hurt you. She'll take your soul and do as she pleases with it. Do you know what that will do to you? You'll be in limbo for eternity. Hell will be like a vacation, and believe me, I know what hell feels like. You want to live forever, don't you?"

"No, I just want to be with Sara." Gabe said and backpedaled some more, feeling with his hands for the doorknob behind him. *Will I ever get to see her again?* Gabe thought.

A heavy downpour, accompanied by thunder and lightning, added to the ferocious winds that had already caused so much damage. Downed lines covered the roads, and trees were ripped out of the ground and thrown like twigs. Houses were smashed open and exposed for all to see. Small debris were blown against fences. It looked as if most of the townspeople stood together in their basements, local schools, and storm cellars. Sara had to be the only person outside in all of Southwick.

"If you decide to go outside, you're probably not going to make it. Touch me and I'll take care of the rest," the tall man said and moved even closer to Gabe. He reached out his skinless arm. Gabe looked away, trying to catch his breath. "All you have to do is touch me." His voice now sounded as if he were talking through an echo chamber. "Soon my form will be totally unrecognizable— my life will cease to exist, as well as yours. Think of what you're passing up."

"I'll never let you touch me. I'd rather die," Gabe said. His back grazed the door.

"You're a fool." The tall man lunged at Gabe. "All you have to do is touch me."

Gabe blinked and saw a face he hadn't see since he was seven years old. "*Dad*," he said and shook his head. *I must be dead*, he thought, blinking.

###

Sara was only a block away from the hotel, but the old truck was starting to sputter and buck. "Damn it, not now!" she yelled, pounding the dashboard. The truck bucked, kicked, and stalled in the middle of the street. She sat there a good thirty seconds, trying to start it. But it was useless—the truck wouldn't start. Tears streamed down her face, and she wiped them away to see. She stumbled out and walked the rest of the way to the hotel.

###

"I know it's you, so stop it." The tall man's face changed back to the rotted look it had before.

He reached for Gabe as if in a last-ditch effort. Gabe turned around and grabbed the door, but there was so much wind pulling that it wouldn't budge. With both hands, he turned the handle and pulled with all his strength, and the hotel door opened, but the wind changed directions and pushed it forward. Gabe fell to the ground, banging his left shoulder and scraping his knee. He was oblivious to the pain in his shoulder and scrambled to get up.

"Come back, Gabe. Please come back. Don't leave me here," the tall man said. Gabe looked over his shoulder and saw the tall man's entire decrepit body. It looked more decomposed than warm living flesh. Pieces of gray skin were falling off and muscle-like fresh meat could be seen. Blood dripped and veins were sticking out. Gabe shrieked and looked away.

Gabe turned and saw Sara who was now no more than fifty feet from him. "Gabe!" she called out as loudly as she could. "Gabe, it's me, Sara!" she yelled again and waved in his direction

The tall man staggered after him. He reached for Gabe and grazed his back. Gabe screamed and his face twisted.

"Gabe, get away from him. Run, Gabe, and don't let him touch you again."

But he did, and Gabe was powerless to move away. It felt as if he didn't have the energy to pick up a pencil and write his own name. His face metamorphosed into that of the tall man's. Sara looked away.

With the wind at her back, she stopped, stretched her arms, and looked toward the swirling, darkened sky. Her hair blew about her face. "No, not again! I don't want to leave this body! Do you hear me?" she screamed louder than exploding bombs. Thunder cracked and bolts of bright lightning flashed, knocking Sara to the ground.

Just think about Sara and how her hair looks in the sun. How her smile made me feel so happy.

"What you're trying to do is useless. You are now mine," the tall man told Gabe.

"Keep fighting, Gabe. You're almost there. That's it, keep doing it."

"Sara?" Gabe said and caught a glimpse of her. His heart thumped, and his face transformed back to the Gabe she loved. He looked at Sara and did exactly what she had said, and forced John's soul out of his body.

"Nooooooo. Noooooooooo. You can't do this," the tall man screamed.

Bluish-white bolts of lightning came out of the ground, and black birds from the sky. He looked up at them. Thousands, perhaps millions, of feathers ruffled, and the tall man screamed again. Gabe covered his ears and closed his eyes. The birds picked up what was left of John and flew away with him. Bluish-white bolts of lightning sparked, and his horrid screams could still be heard. Thunder cracked and a bolt of lightning flashed. Gabe opened his eyes and watched in horror with his mouth wide open and his hair blowing all over his face.

EPILOGUE

Three days after the storm

Gabe had just gotten out of the shower at a friend's house and was drying himself off. On the back of the bathroom door hung a full-length mirror. He glanced at it, and to his surprise, Sara's face gazed back at him, just like it had when he had looked at the water in the lake a few days ago.

He dropped the towel and walked to the mirror. "I must be going crazy." He closed his eyes, and when he opened them, all he saw was his own reflection. "The windmill, I must go to the windmill."

Gabe quickly dressed and headed over to Sara's house, even though in less than a few hours his mother was going to be buried at the Edgewood Cemetery.

The sun shone without a cloud in the sky. A rich blue hovered over the community of Southwick. The townspeople worked side by side, trying to put back together their broken town. The old gray slate roof at the local church, which stood for eighty-five years, had been split open, but they still would have Sunday morning mass there. It didn't matter that the town was in pieces—it would be packed like never before with people waiting to hear Father Honeycomb's sermon.

Driving around fallen lampposts, abandoned cars, and smaller debris, Gabe couldn't help but think about what happened in the mirror. He slowed up when he saw the museum, which was the only building in Southwick that didn't show a sign of the biggest storm of the century. He pulled over, parked the car, and rolled down the window. When he thought about Sara, he smiled. A warm feeling filled his body. He shivered. In the background, he could hear the church bell ringing like a beacon of hope.

When he reached Sara's house, her father was standing out front by his old car. Gabe parked across the street and slowly walked up to him.

Johnny looked up and said, "*Sara.*" He shook his head and blinked his eyes. He eyed Gabe and put a dirty rag in his back pocket. "I'm sorry to hear about your mother, Gabe." He still eyed him and shook his head.

"Thanks, Mr. Livingston," Gabe said and kicked at the ground. "I see you're working on the car."

"Yeah." He looked at it. "I'll see what I can do."

"I'm sure you'll do a good job. And if I can, I'll drop by this weekend."

"Thanks. Have you heard from Sara?" Mr. Livingston asked.

Gabe shook his head and looked toward the sky. "No, I haven't but I bet she's out there somewhere."

Mr. Livingston took a deep breath. "You've got that right."

"I was wondering if I could have a look at the old windmill behind your house?"

"You mean the place Sara used to always go?" His eyebrows arched. "Yeah."

"Sure, if you'd like to, go ahead." He shook his head. "I know what you're thinking, but that was the first place I checked when Sara didn't come home."

"Thanks, Mr. Livingston. It'll only be a few minutes."

Gabe hurried across the yard, through the dirt path, and finally to the old windmill. The moment he spotted it, he stopped and stared. He figured the storm would have leveled it to pieces, but there it stood as it had on the night he had first seen it. Gabe cautiously walked into the windmill, but nothing happened—no visions, voices, or smells this time. Gabe moved all the way in. Bright yellow light suddenly appeared, lightening the inside of the windmill. Right before his eyes, Sara slid out of his body and stood right across from him with a hazy yellowish glow around her.

"Sara, my God, is that you?" Gabe said and reached out to touch her.

"It's a reflection of my spirit that you're seeing. I'm sorry for what happened. I would have never jumped into your body without asking, but I had no choice."

"I guess we'll never get to go to that school dance you asked me to."

"No, I'm afraid not." She looked away.

"You saved me, Sara, didn't you?"

She shook her head. "In a way, but you saved me too. You helped me to understand why I have to continue to do what I do. You don't know how much I wish we could be together."

"You don't have to say any more. We were only together for a little while, but it was the best time of my life—a time I'll cherish forever, but what about me? I wanted to be like you." Gabe's eyes locked on hers.

"That can never be, but together we can be Gabe Chaplin, the painter. Isn't that what you wanted before you met me?"

"Yes, all I ever wanted to be was a painter." Suddenly overcome with emotion, his eyes watered.

"Don't cry, Gabe. And remember to enjoy life. It's the most precious thing we have."

Sara's reflection started to fade and the lights with her. Without warning, a black bird with a gray tuft of hair on the top of its head flew out of the windmill. Gabe brought his arms over his head protectively, but then dropped them, smiled, and watched the bird fly away.